"*The Longcut*, Emily Hall's debut fiction, is about nothing less than that elusive subject: art. Sinuous sentences slyly wind their way around that vexing question: Art, what is it? Unexpected, provocative answers follow in this ambitious fiction."

—Christine Schutt, *Pure Hollywood*

"The anxieties of the artist are vigorously analyzed to the point of near insanity in Emily Hall's schizophrenic debut. An artist walks through a city to an appointment, asking the simple and unanswerable question: what is my work? Hilarious and claustrophobic, angular and digressive, *The Longcut* questions the role of capitalism in creation, while proving it's nearly impossible to make art if one thinks about it too much."

—Mark Haber, *Reinhardt's Garden*

"*The Longcut* is a funny, serious, spiky, and very stylish philosophical object that leads the reader into and out of absurdity and toward something like freedom. I loved this book."

—Christine Smallwood, *The Life of the Mind*

"If the narrator of this stellar debut novel read this blurb, she would probably categorize it as *blurb, metacommentary in the form of.* Or if I wrote '*The Loser* by Thomas Bernhard but about art,' she would probably categorize it as *blurb, name dropping and/or influence of.* Or if I wrote 'the most fun I've had reading a cognitive apparatus in action, novel in the form of,' she would probably categorize it as *category, categorization of categorization of.*"

—Mauro Javier Cárdenas, *Aphasia*

Emily Hall

THE LONGCUT

DALKEY ARCHIVE PRESS

Dallas / Dublin

Library of Congress Control Number: 2022931017

ISBN: 978-1-62897-397-6 (paperback)

ISBN: 978-1-62897-416-4 (ebook)

Cover and exterior design by Evan Sult

Dalkey Archive Press

Dallas/Dublin

www.dalkeyarchive.com

For
Nate

Ros: We could play at questions.

Guil: What good would that do?

—Tom Stoppard, *Rosencrantz & Guildenstern Are Dead*

The Longcut

I was always asking myself what my work was, I thought as I walked to the gallery. As an artist I knew I should know what my work was, I thought as I walked, still I did not know what my work was, could not stop asking myself what my work was, it being impossible to think about anything else. It being acceptable as it was for an artist in my time to make art from anything, with anything, about anything, the world constituting the art world in my time being undelimited in a liberating or terrifying manner, still I could not stop asking myself what my work was, even as I told myself I really should already know the answer. Still there was never any question of the question, it remained an open question, the question of what my work was, which is to say how would I know my work when my work presented itself to me.

Walking from street to street in the city to a gallery for a meeting with a gallery person—a *gallerist*, a word I could not or would not say—I continued asking myself what my work was, how I might discuss my work, whatever it was, at this meeting set up by my friend the well-known artist who set up situations. This meeting not being, as it was not, a situation that could be said to be part of my friend's well-known artwork of setting up situations, even as he had in fact set it—the meeting—up, the meeting unrelated to his work being in fact a meeting related somehow, in some manner, to mine.

When I had called her—the *gallerist*—to arrange the meeting set up by my friend the well-known artist who set up situations, this call taking place the morning post a drinks appointment with him at a rooftop bar, she—the gallerist—had hailed me on the telephone in a hoarse manner, her hailing taking place under hoarse voice conditions. Having delayed and delayed and delayed, I had eventually called this hoarse gallerist, delaying while imagining and rehearsing numerous and various one-sided conversation scenarios, then permitting myself, instead of calling her, to prepare and eat oatmeal while looking out the window at the bodega and laundry across the street, watching someone coming out of the bodega, taking something out of a bag, eating it. The idea of relaying anything to a person with a gallery showing work by people who knew what their work was too abstract, it abstracted too much information on which my hold was already doubtful, forcing me therefore to cling to the specifics of person eating out of a bag in front of the bodega. We were eating together, that person and

I, but I was the only one knowing it. My one-sided eating event with the person across the street being much like my one-sided conversation with the gallery person, or gallerist, I came to the conclusion that I might as well call her.

What I would tell her was a question.

It was a question, both were questions, requiring time for considering, time for considering being always as it was scarce in the category *time, allotment of in the life of the artist.* The time allotted for the meeting with the gallerist having been achieved by my taking a day off from my job, calling in sick when sick had nothing to do with it, I was thus walking remorsefully to the gallery considering, even as I continued to ask myself what my work was, the likely expression of my boss on my return the next day, my boss having lately been pausing his generally benevolent affect to look at me with a sort of slant through the glass door of his office whenever I passed by. I was not aware of any reason for him to look at me with a sort of slant, whether it had to do with the number of smoking breaks I took during the time allotted or expected for doing the tasks of my job was something he had not relayed to me or had not relayed in any form I recognized. Further I was trying to keep the number of smoking breaks under control, not being, as I was not, in thrall to smoking so much as to the cognitive processes attached to my doing it, it—the smoking break—being my strategy when I was confronted by a question at my job I did not know the answer to, a strategy of going outside for a smoking break at the end of which, owing to some cerebral or cognitive process, I could answer the question and complete it by moving it into the "completed" column, a resolution thus connected to the cigarette, brought about by the cigarette rather than having been brought about by me. The questions at my job I did not know the answer to were different in every aspect from the question of what my work was, being as they were—the job questions—answerable through the strategy of the smoking break, which the answer to the question of what my work was was not. Whether my boss had noticed or clocked the frequency of my smoking breaks was an open question, even as the security guards at the building where my job took place had noticed and clocked, nodding to me in an I-see-you manner whenever I left the building, although certainly the security guards didn't in fact care and only told me please to move away from the building's doorway so as not to turn my smoking break into everyone else's. My boss had not in fact confronted me about my smoking breaks, still however I needed to keep my job, the realities of the category *expenses, pressures of in the life of the artist* being brought to bear as they did on me in the usual ways. Without my job, I was always having to remind myself, the escalation of problems in the category *expenses, pressures of* would leave me little time to answer the question of what my work was. I thus had no plans to abandon my job, even with the questions requiring the cognitive processes of smoking to resolve, no matter how alarming the prospect of the crisped condition of my lungs and no matter how often I was made to move away from the building's entrance by any security guard.

The question of what my work was thus constantly haunting or dogging me, art being as it was something that could be made from anything at all and could be about or relating to anything at all, how therefore, I could not stop asking myself, did you—I—pluck from the stream of life or ideas the contents of your—my—work or the materials with which to do it. I was pulled however hither and yon by the stream of life or ideas, unable to pluck, unable to sort or sift one thing from another, thus the question of what my work was remained an open question, nothing in the other parts of my life having provided a model for or example of how I might close it, the smoking breaks closing the questions I could not answer at my job being not quite the thing. Further I was hampered or dogged by my mental maneuverings, not being able to stop myself, as I was not, following words wherever they went, not being able to stop myself falling into any ferret hole that presented itself, even as I had somehow learned at some point that ferrets preferred not to dig their own holes but took over instead the holes of others, in any case I was forced to follow any idea or reference down any ferret hole it wanted to take over and try out or else to abandon it—the idea or reference—entirely, some other idea having hijacked my cognitive apparatus, and hope to eventually track down laboriously the first idea in whichever ferret hole I had left it and bring it to its logical conclusion. Logical conclusions rarely being of course available, still I tried. My rarely being able to bring any idea to a logical conclusion being more or less a point of fact. It being always of course possible, it continued being possible, that some idea had continued to vectorially travel on its own without me and was no longer in whichever ferret hole I had last seen it, if I could hope even to remember where that was, it being possible that due to mental maneuverings on some other idea, related distantly but distinctly in a manner I would have to laboriously rediscover, the idea would have decided or been forced to travel on a different vector, or else the location of the ferret hole would have moved, shunted off to someplace not previously represented on the map. Still, often I could not remember my first idea anyway, even laboriously tracking back through all the various hijackings and ferret holes, my cognitive apparatus yanking me hither and yon, tossing me about as if in a clothes dryer, with the additional problem of the apparatus producing the activity being both the thing doing the tossing and the thing tossed. Of being both the fishhook and the lip. Many ideas sometimes having been lost entirely, they in fact, in odd moments, popped up in new guises that I amnesiatically assumed to be something entirely else. The question of what my work was—to say nothing of the ferret holes—kept me awake at night, whether I made the correct preparations for sleep or threw myself into bed like an undergraduate. A smoking break would do nothing to remedy the situation, in any case a smoking break when I was not at my job was not a smoking break but merely smoking.

My spending the whole of the night picking up and discarding possibilities or working through the possibilities presented by the philosophical objects I was already making but which didn't answer the question of what my work was left me exhausted at my job on mornings that followed, left me confronted with questions I might ordinarily be able to answer had I not been kept awake all night by the question of what my work was, thus requiring more smoking breaks and thus more slant looks from my boss through the glass door of his office when I returned from my cognitive encounter with the cigarette. My understanding having been previously that he didn't care how many smoking breaks I took so long as I answered my share of questions and moved them into the "completed" column, I was nevertheless eventually forced to admit that perhaps my understanding was wrong, that it was mis-, I was forced to admit that perhaps he might care after all, thus requiring me as well to care and to get my smoking breaks under control, the way to do this being finally to figure out the answer to the question of what my work was and start to do it.

In any case, even were the question of what my work was to be answered, still I would need my job, owing to the realities of the category *expenses, pressures of in the life of the artist* and owing as well to the urgency of keeping myself from polluting the answer to the question of what my work was with considerations of the economic market. Thus it had seemed to me for a time to be efficient to try combining my work with my job, I recalled as I walked to the gallery meeting, by making work out of the tasks or tools of my job—answering questions and moving them into the "completed" column—thus letting my job bear or siphon off any urgency about the category *expenses, pressures of* or considerations of the economic market, to make my job both the source of the disquiet and the method of alleviating it, my job thus resembling one of those deadlocked puzzles, there not existing without the irritant the art. Which is to say, to make my job my patron.

In any case in the category *expenses, pressures of in the life of the artist*, there were scant funds to be used in the category *materials, possible*. My patron,

I had thought, I recalled as I walked to the gallery, could perhaps be persuaded to look the other way as I pilfered some thumbtacks and a roll of tape.

Whether I had this—my job, my patron—in mind when I began bringing the egg to my job every day was a question among other questions all the while presenting themselves to me as I hauled myself hither and yon, including what was Cambridge blue, why was no aria by Handel as beautiful as "Forte e lieto," what was difference between *perhaps* and *maybe*, when did a handshake begin and end. Did a handshake begin with the meeting of hands or did it begin with the idea presenting itself of wanting to meet a person in handshake friendliness. Did it end when a person became someone whose hand you no longer wanted to meet with yours.

The egg was not a real egg but one made of granite or marble or something made to look it, heavy in the hand and given to me be an aunt now deceased, its color grayish blue with flecks of black and other blue as well as flecks of something that flickered and shone and changed color, making me feel numerous and various ways depending on the time of day or the amount of light in the room. It—the egg—was kept in a box at the foot of my bed with other objects and clipped-out articles that, like the egg, did not comply or complied poorly with known categories, a box usually piled over with books and with further clipped-out articles and papers belonging to known categories such as *bills* or *medical advice, not yet taken* but that I did not feel like filing or putting away for various reasons including laziness. The box of noncompliant things had an air of uneasiness or rather I was not easy with it, the air of uneasiness as I looked at and through it being mine, I had eventually understood, feeling as I did or seeming as I was permeable to the airs and feelings of others not limited to people but including objects, or else the objects being permeable to my airs, taking them, willingly or unwillingly, on. I was certainly prone to think a great deal at that time when considering my philosophical objects about whether things fit perfectly into known categories, categories that could be listed and pronounced and sequenced, or whether they flew or flitted between them depending on the time of day and the amount of light in the room. The egg being an uneasy object, a thing with weight and color, still what was it really. Was an egg not a real egg because it couldn't be eaten. It belonged, I was often forced to admit, to some known categories, to the category *gifts from relatives, deceased*, but whether it belonged to the category *objects, good to look at* was unclear, being as it was that certainly sometimes I liked to look at the egg and sometimes I shoved it back into the box and re-piled the books and compliant papers on top, forcing myself then to think about anything else. It certainly did not belong to the category *fire, things I would risk my life for in a*, I would not have run back into a burning building to pop it in my pocket, certainly however, at the same time it did not belong to the category *chuck, things I could easily*, especially when the sunlight moved across the room in a certain way. Thus the condition of having no category or known sequence of categories kept me from chucking the articles and objects but it did not prevent me entering a zone of not understanding what I was looking at, further keeping me in the zone of thinking about zones, even as I had found myself in or remained in those zones for years or more.

The idea of pursuing the truth of the egg's category and its relationship to other philosophical objects had led me to pop it—the egg—in my pocket and carry it to my job and put it on a ledge that happened to be attached to a wall near my desk unit, the egg thus being lit up in bright everyday light entering through windows that began by my feet at the floor. The desk unit was not in fact my regular desk unit, being as it was a temporary desk unit I had been moved to by my boss while some repair was being done on a vent over the location of my usual moving of items into the "completed" column. I'm sorry about this, he had said on the day he moved me, he had been really very sorry and indeed had looked a bit sorry, not knowing, as he had not, how long this situation or condition would go on. Thus was the new desk unit a spatiotemporal unknown, its zone of spatiotemporal unknowability being perhaps a factor in my idea of putting the egg on a ledge in order to observe it, an object from an uncategorized zone dwelling in a zone of spatiotemporal unknowability. I thought, that is to say, that I could find out if the zone of not understanding what I was looking at extended in some manner from the foot of my bed to my job, whether it could be said to be a zone of place or a zone of time or a zone of something belonging to the object, something about the truth of the object or its categories, a quality or set of qualities jolted into clarity by the instability of the spatiotemporal unknown. Thus it was impossible to avoid the zone of thinking about zones, the zone of my job thus possibly constituting, as it might, a zone linked to the zone of the foot of my bed by various zones of varying concrete condition. Thus the egg became a double agent crossing the borders of zones, working as it did against the foot of my bed while at my job or working against my job while at the foot of my bed. What the zones of other artists were was an open question, the zone worked in by my friend the well-known artist who set up situations seeming to me to be a zone of self-contained clarity, a zone in which there was never any unclarity about what his work was, his work of setting up situations and seeing what followed.

At the spatiotemporal unknown I popped the egg

out of my pocket and put it on the ledge—a ledge
not connected to the desk unit or the window or
anything I could identify, a ledge dwelling in the categories *architectural features, purpose of unknown* and
office space, unclaimed territories in—and observed it
often throughout the day to see what came up, the
observing being an action I was forced to undertake
on the sly, the ledge being as it was in the direct line
of sight of the glass door of my boss's office. My boss
being thus able to look over the ledge at me at any
time of day with any kind of slant he liked. Thus as
I observed the egg often throughout the day, I found
myself observing as well the face of my boss to see if
he was looking at me with a sort of slant and to see if
it thus was time to buckle down and move items into
the "completed" column in an expedited manner in
order to keep my job and not trouble the category
expenses, pressures of, the egg thus also taking on the
double-agent assignment of helping me to answer
the question of what my work was and at the same
time to keep my job as I did.

I walked to the gallery recalling that at the end
of the first day of observing the egg between, as
best I could, the slant looks of my boss, time having passed, it had not been clear to me whether the
egg should be popped back in my pocket and taken
back from the zone of my desk unit to the zone at
the foot of my bed, if it had passed sufficient time
on the ledge with no identifiable purpose adjacent

to the spatiotemporal unknown in my office to acquire or signal or be coaxed toward a new zone or a zone I could perceive, or toward a new context, this—*context*—being a word used often by my friend the downtown professor of visual and media studies, *context* being a word with some microsliver of difference from the word *zone* that I was in that immediate moment unable to identify. It had not been clear to me whether the coaxing was the case, I recalled as I turned a corner by a pipe liberating steam from somewhere deeply below the street, a sign propped next to it reading *raise plow*. It had not been clear to me whether the egg needed more time at my job, unruptured by evenings and nights in the box at the foot of my bed, its place of origin, in order to continue its work as a double agent. And further what if I forgot to take it out of my pocket on any morning or if I troubled the timeline by having dinner appointments with my friend the well-known artist who set up situations or others. I then more or less understood that an egg spending a day on the ledge near my desk might discover one kind of zone or context or truth, a visiting context, whereas however an egg spending two days on the ledge near my desk might discover another and so forth, especially if the light moved across the room in a certain way, eventually perhaps becoming something that belonged to the zone of my job instead of my apartment, glued into context on the ledge near my desk unit as something I could come to ignore. I saw, that is to say, that it was never going to be possible to know the truth about any object.

How did other artists discover the truth about any object or in fact answer the question of what their work was, I asked myself near raise plow, nearly walking into a person crossing the street in front of me. Did other artists ask the same questions or did they ask the same questions in different words, both of these being questions that opened up into other questions, spatchcocked questions revealing spatch-cocked others. Whether their—the artists'—pursuit of their work or the question of what their work was was more serious than mine was a problem or question that dogged me: was I fundamentally unse-rious, I was haunted by thinking, was my pursuit a joke, even as the border between serious work and joke-seeming work was transparent seeming and permeable, joke-seeming work being a zone easy to cross into without knowing it. Or for some artists, it must be said, without caring. The truth was that I had no way of gauging my seriousness or unserious-ness, I was forced to admit near the steam and raise plow, my seriousness being a variable or provisional sense causing me thus on some days to seem serious to myself while on others the reverse seemed equally or exclusively true, my serious-seeming enquiry into the question of what my work was seeming to oth-ers to be flakiness, a failure to buckle down, to be

dicking around, as another friend, a British printmaker, would say, *dicking around* being what she
had called it in her blunt conversational style. Even
as buckling down or stopping dicking around before
I had the answer to the question of what my work
was seemed fatal. What indeed if I buckled myself
to the wrong thing or mistranslated a correct thing
into the wrong material. At some point later, on a
particular day between other days, I had put into
motion the idea of not just observing but photographing the egg in various contexts, thinking at
that time that photography might reveal the truth
about any object, or that photography plus time
would reveal it, this being something that could be
said to have come out of my observations about photography, about the difference between the world
and the photographed world, this seeming to me
to be a serious enquiry, this seeming to me to be
something that could be said about a serious enquiry
but probably not something that would be said by
serious artist-photographers or the serious artist-photographers I happened to know. Where would I go
to meet some unserious or appropriately less serious
artist-photographers, I had found myself considering at the time, I recalled as I walked.

Near raise plow I then recalled the idea for the
impossible project, the projecting project that had
occurred to me after a dinner-date appointment
with my friend the well-known artist who set

up situations, a project in which I would project myself into the lives of other artists. The dinner-date appointment took place at a restaurant as sleek and calm and minimal as my friend, where we seemed to be the only people in the room, even as the room was full of calm and sleek people murmuring to other calm and sleek people about ideas and news brought to the surface of the stream of life from somewhere unknowable deeply below. I asked myself, had asked myself at the time and before and after, what would breach my friend's calm, private, self-contained air and minimalist lifestyle, his giving little away while still being a true friend and comrade in my search for the answer to the question of what my work was, even as I suspected that even were it possible to breach his calm, private exterior, I would find underneath another layer of calm, private, minimalist self, also difficult to breach.

We seemed by virtue of friendship and conversation to find ourselves in a spotlight in an otherwise dark room, even as this was not true, not absolutely true.

Even as I knew he would never answer the question of what my work was in any direct manner, nevertheless I could not help myself asking him what he thought the answer might be. Nevertheless in asking him and hearing the same answer I had heard before, more or less, the answer being *you tell me* told to me in different syntactical constructions,

I had in that immediate moment of the dinner, thinking how unlike were my exterior and layers and his, understood that I could at least minimally delimit what my work was not. I did not want to set up situations, rather what I wanted was his self-contained air of certainty, the calm that concealed calm. As we shared a plate of whelks in butter I could not prevent myself asking myself whether acquiring his minimalist lifestyle would lend me, too, his self-contained air of certainty and clarity, leading me to be able to breach the border of the realm of not knowing what my work was. I could not stop myself imagining inhabiting his life and seeing where it led. It was then in that immediate moment of the whelks in butter that the idea presented itself to me for the impossible project, the projecting project, of inhabiting the lives of other artists. Could I find out the answer to the question of what my work was by inhabiting for a month or years the lives of artists I admired, I considered as I slipped whelks from their shells, seeing if the result was work like theirs or something else. Could I figure out what my work was, that is to say, by hurling or aiming myself like a projectile at the work of others.

Even as I knew that the project of projecting myself into the lives of others was an impossible project—the logistics being situated as they were in the category of *projects, impossible*—a joke project from a skit about serious but bad artists, a project likely as not to immediately be consigned to the category *joke project, not to be considered*, still I enjoyed imagining it, could not prevent myself imagining undertaking it, producing as it did an odd sort of pleasure for my cognitive apparatus, a mental maneuvering producing a woken-up feeling of meaning and possibility and spiking out in time, even as I could not in that moment have said what it was. Relaying however the impossible idea to my calm friend with the minimalist lifestyle and the well-known work of setting up situations, after the whelk shells had been whisked away by a serene and confident waiter, I found him enthusiastic about the projecting project in his way, in his calm way, it— the impossible project—being for him not a joke project from a skit but one calmly and distantly related, by marriage or nodding acquaintance-ship, to the work of setting up situations. Many situations having their origins, he said in his calm way, toying in an abstract manner with a whelk shell he had abstracted from the plate prior to the plate's being serenely whisked away, in the category of *thought experiment*, which was the category he smoothly assigned to it. This projecting project, he had thought and said, I recalled by raise plow, could be called or bent back from the category *joke project, not to be considered* toward something like perfor-mance in the category *thought experiment, origins in*. You're being too literal, he told me during our

dinner-date appointment, he had said in his calm
mystifying way.

The impossible project didn't have to be a literal
inhabiting, I later decided, drawing up and pinning
to the walls of my so-called studio, a.k.a. my apartment, lists of artists I admired and their qualities, it
could be an approximation, I decided, I could carry
it out by approximating. Thinking about the conditions and qualities of their lives and selves, of artists
living and dead who knew what their work was and
were doing or had done it, I imagined approximately
re-creating them—the conditions—in order to see
whether they would lead to their work or something
else. Did the life produce the work seemed to be
the question. Did conditions produce the thinking, further which conditions turned thought into
action, also where, it occurred to me as I considered
and drew up and pinned, did the borders of art
touch and bend away from the sociological experiment. Knowing of course that external conditions
were only part of the answer to the question of what
anyone's work was, I was further not interested par-
ticularly in inhabiting the mentalities or sensibilities of others, in any case my own mentality would
almost certainly fling itself at any mentality I tried
to inhabit, the mentalities thus finding themselves
stuck together as with mousetrap glue or else the one
jammed in the doorway of the other like a wedge.
On the other hand I would almost certainly not

be able to prevent myself thinking about the work of artists whose lives and qualities I was approximating inhabiting, even as I was not interested in inhabiting their mentalities or sensibilities, such a sustained meditation being almost certain to cause a leak or transfer into my own mentality or sensibility, the border of the realm of my own sensibility being as it was at times permeable or provisional, too much so in my opinion but also perhaps useful for information gathering toward finding out or discovering what my work was. Except when it wasn't. In any case the impossible project resembled in a fashion the photographing of the egg in a different context, in this case the context being the lives of others and the egg being me. A context might be a newborn child, my equivalences being getting up every two hours at night and doing something urgent, as I imagined the artist-mother of the newborn child having to do every two hours with the newborn child, learning about architecture in the style of Soviet brutalism in a stop-and-start manner, as the artist-mother of the newborn child had done during infant naps in order to do her work about various bodies occupying various architectural forms and the political qualities transferred from one to the other, eating vegan food requiring trips to food shops beyond the usual map, thus approximating, that is to say, what I understood to be the elements she negotiated into the category *time, allotment of in the life of the artist.* These equivalences allowing me, as they would, to forgo producing a newborn child for the project, thus not forcing me to cross the border of the moral limits as I understood them or go beyond the pale as I understood the pale. The artist with the newborn child would be the context and I would be the thing put into it, it also seeming true in that case that I would be the context into which I put her life and qualities to see what came out of it. Perhaps I would discover which of us was object and which was context, with the results of that portion of the impossible project put into some form possibly like a lab report. Having subsequent to the drawing and pinning up that same day brought myself and the egg to my job, I became aware that the woken-up feeling was leading to a feeling of frenzy coming on as I thought about approximating or establishing equivalences or equivalents, even as the glare of the frenzy was nicked slightly as I recalled the task of moving things into the "completed" column and was forced to consider where in the category *time, allotment of in the life of the artist.* I would be imagining and executing equivalences for the lives of artists I admired, not to mention observing the egg on the ledge near my desk unit, not to mention doing my job. The frenzy was further nicked and slightly overcast by my abruptly registering a task I had ceased to do, sitting at my desk as though moving things into the "completed" column but in fact actually not. How on earth could a person have time for all this was something I often considered at that and every time.

The observing and later photographing of the egg not being in fact the first covert actions undertaken at my job, I reminded myself as I walked to the gallery, the covert actions having been for a time an ongoing pursuit. There were the tiny pin-prick circles I drew in an endless manner on narrow strips of paper abstracted from the overflow bin of the office paper shredder—the paper shredder being an endless mechanism, I later understood, for moving documents into the category *defunct* or else relieving them of their categories for good—the pin-prick circles clustering and covering the strips of paper like the metastasizing cells I hoped were not in or gearing themselves up for my lungs. My drawing endlessly of the pin-prick circles had been part of the despairing or demented attempt to make work at my job, my demented attempt to make my job my patron at a time when the elements of the category *funds, allotment of in the life of the artist* were insufficient for the purchase of materials, the drawing thus being another action I was performing frugally or covertly or on the sly, even as it was easier than the subsequent action of observing the egg on the ledge near my desk unit, being as it was—the drawing—an action I could perform bent tensely over as if moving items into the "completed" column and thus not attracting the attention of my boss at that moment or time from a distance at least. My drawing of cancerous pin-prick circles had been in fact also part of a doomed attempt to quit smoking, to discover an activity that would take the place of the smoking break in leading me to the answer to questions that presented themselves to me that I could not answer, an activity that would resultantly take me less often past the glass door of my boss's office and his slant looks, thus a double-agent action or activity helping me to do two things at once, or three if I counted, which I was forced to do, not encouraging or amplifying the cells gearing themselves up in my lungs. The covered strips of paper became compelling objects, worn soft and dented with different kinds of pen, objects that I would later understand to have changed category from *materials, castoff* to *materials, picked up*, from *defunct* to *quick*, but which at the time I recognized only as a sly action performed in odd moments of time stolen from my job, performed in stolen time. Using, for that matter, stolen materials. Had I understood at the time their category transfer or movement, I would have thus differently understood my tender attention to the flow of trash from my job to my work, whatever it turned out to be. Time having passed, my boss approached my desk unit and asked me please to refrain from abstracting strips of paper from the shredder, the strips of paper in the

shredder's outflow bin being as they were destined
for whisking away periodically by a high-security
information-disposal firm and not for being covered
on the sly with pin-prick circles. Not having shown
him any strips of paper covered in pin-prick circles,
I could only conclude that I had not been as sly or
covert as I imagined, I could only conclude that
he had noticed me abstracting or covering, I could
only conclude—again—that he in fact noticed more
than I thought. My boss having asked me to confine
my activity—my abstracting activity rather than my
activity of moving items to the "completed" column—to any torn-up scraps of paper I liked which
were not in the shredder, I replied that I would.
Certainly, I told him. Ok good, he said. In any case
the cancerous pin-prick circles on shreds of paper
had not managed to take the place of the smoking
break, I thought as I walked to the gallery, being as
I was too compelled by them.

I tried subsequently in fact continuing drawing pin-prick circles endlessly in the evening in my
so-called studio, a.k.a. my apartment, on scraps of
paper taken from various outflow bins not destined
for whisking away and portaged home in my pockets. These actions being interpretable as the producing and observing of circles in different zones, however, in fact, in my so-called studio post my job in
the evenings the endless cancerous pin-prick circles
went flat, whether drawn on the back of a discarded

overdue gas-bill envelope from an outflow bin in my so-called studio or on any torn-up scrap of paper from my job which I had jammed in my pocket at the end of the day. I eventually understood that the cancerous pin-prick circles had withered removed from their condition as attempted strategies for addressing questions to which I did not know the answers. They had withered in my so-called studio, they had withered out of context, the original paper strips taken from the shredder's outflow bin and drawn on at my desk at my job withering, the torn-up scraps jammed in my pocket at the end of the day withering, the gas-bill envelope producing nothing at all. They all became less interesting, being as they were, I then or eventually understood, in the wrong context, either viewed in the wrong zone or produced in the wrong zone, the conditions of secrecy and pilfering that had charged with energy the strips of paper from the shredder's outflow bin not being possible to replicate in unstolen time in my so-called studio, not replicable by the torn-up sheets authorized by my boss with only the merest, relatively, it should be said, slant. Out their zones or context the objects became failed objects, being as they were unrelated to production and labor, the conditions of my job, of moving items into the "completed" column, thus constituting objects I had to admit I did not care for. I was not mad keen for objects made in unstolen time, in time that was not

stolen from my job. Further I did not understand
how I might go about replicating the conditions or
context in which they would not wither, stealthily or
absurdly bringing for example nonjob people to my
job and office—who those nonjob people might be
being an open question—to secretly view the paper
shreds or secretly view my drawing on them in stolen time, such an action being, as it was, beyond
the pale. Even as I knew that the pale was merely a
territory marked out by the artist, a set of borders or
zones she set down according to her own lights and
then forced others into avoiding or crossing, even
as I knew that in this case absurdly bringing people
to my office to view the shreds of paper would or
might constitute a brave outflinging of the border
or my own personal pale, a pale I was in any case
not brave enough to outfling or claim. The establishment or violation of the pale being, I had often
thought, I recalled on my way to the gallery, the
point, even as I knew that for other artists there were
other points, I recalled as I walked, the question of
points in any case itself being open, there being no
probability of a truth or constant relating to any
point from one artist to another.

Was there ever such thing as a constant, I had
often asked myself, I thought for the eight millionth
time at the time as I walked to the gallery, and how
far into the indefinite future would observing the
egg and so forth be necessary to determine it. How

long did it take to think about things eight million times was also a question. Time was always a question, not only in the category *time, allotment of in the life of the artist* but also in the category *time, understanding the passage of,* time also being as it was at the same time a powerful subject for art and a time-worn one, and also as well an element I was forced to consider as I threw myself into my job garments on mornings among other mornings, having missed the appropriate moment for dressing and leaving my so-called studio, having lost track of time considering timeworn subjects, not even, it must be said, in that case, on that morning or others like it, dressed or prepared with clean face and teeth. Bringing my focus to bear on the immediate moment one morning, gulping some cold coffee and dashing water on my face, I had been all the while asking myself how on earth a person could get everything done in a day or in a few hours before going to her job, even sans observing an egg or approximating the conditions or qualities of the lives of other artists, thus finding myself led again to the category *time, understanding the passage of* as I brushed my teeth without noticing myself do it. Thus again was the border of the realm of my cognitive space permeable and porous, I could not keep myself or other things out of it, thus was the border of the realm of the immediate moment so porous I could not keep myself in. Time, I had considered as I threw myself into my not exceedingly clean job garments, was in a way the subject of any art, there being time elapsed between the making of the art by one person and the seeing of it by another, even a microsliver of time between action and perception, there being time elapsed, years or lifetimes, between seeing it the first time and seeing it again, with elements in the category *time, passage of* working on both viewer and art so that nothing was ever the same twice, even a feeling referring to a feeling from yesterday or long ago or in a dream. And seeing being only part of it, you passed your body through the work or bent your mind around it while remembering the last time you passed through or bent around, perhaps the last time you moved your body through or around this work you were with your wife, now your ex-wife, you now have a limp, now the haze of depression has lifted and you are walking with a livelier step, even with your limp. Time being as it was a timeworn subject, I recalled asking myself as I threw myself into my job garments, why was it we were still so surprised by the actions in the category *time, passage of* in any form. In any case, I recalled as I walked, it had then been a case on that morning of it being time to hurl myself out of my building and toward my job, where it would then be time to answer the questions that presented themselves and to move items into the "completed" column instead of trying to answer the question of what

my work was. Clinging to a pole in a subway car on
many mornings, I recalled as I walked, I had found
myself considering the depressing ways in which
the tasks of my job, answering questions and moving items into the "completed" column, of moving
items between categories, could be said to constitute
a system for marking or patrolling time, a system
possibly in aid of the category *time, understanding
the passage of,* although in an entirely depressing
manner. Moreover this system, it could be said—
enforcing the not-flitting of items into errant categories, a flitting they seemed not to be able to stop
themselves attempting but which was nevertheless
thwarted by my smoking breaks, so that an item was
resultantly "completed" or not, a question answered
or not—was invented or intended to keep time moving steadily into the "completed" column, forward-
ing along without hiccupping or stalling or falling
into a dead faint. My job system, it could be said,
was meant to annihilate the hiccups caused by category confusion, no matter how often a question I
could not immediately answer presented itself, these
not being changeable conditions if the sunlight happened to lurch across the office in a compelling way
over a few hours in the afternoon or if the sky went
suddenly dark. Which is to say that an item that did
not eventually move into the "completed" column
was understood to be an impossible thing, a null
category, a category in which I supposed time would

collapse and my boss would look slant to a degree from which he would never recover.

Wait, I recalled myself thinking as I clung to the pole and the train had ceased hurtling between stations on that morning or too many others like it, the train having stopped in an abrupt manner between stations with a smell of brakes rising and the interior lights flickering like a migraine, this was not the case, it was un-, there was a "pending" column suspended between "new" and "completed," although "pending" was a column I had come to not see, not being, as I was not, permitted to use it. I had consigned it to the category *ignore, things I could or did*, the column "pending" being as it was irrelevant to my task of moving items into the "completed" column, being as it was—the "pending" column—for the use of bosses only, "pending," should I attempt using it, likely to result in something more serious than a slant look from my boss. I ignored it, that is to say, until I no longer saw it. Considering as I walked to the gallery what "pending" might officially mean, I supposed that in the absence of being allowed to use it I had created my own strategy for "pending," that is to say the smoking break and the concomitant or subsequent cerebral or cognitive process. What strategies other people at my job might have invented for "pending" was an open question, whether other people at my job invented strategies for fiddling around between

categories, between "new" and "completed," was
an open question, whether other people at my job
were fiddling or in fact permitted to use "pending,"
and was "pending" forbidden only to me. What was
the truth about "pending," I recalled thinking as I
walked to the gallery.

Perhaps the truth about "pending," or any object,
could be seen in or through a photograph, I had
thought at some point between one thing and
another, I recalled as I walked, a park coming up in
my immediate future. Having thought about photographing the egg for various days without doing it—
being as it was necessary to determine the best time
of day for photographing, the light bouncing differently off or suffusing the surface of the egg at different times of day and my boss being more or less
attentive at others—I often missed the moment for
photographing it, continuing to ask myself whether
a better moment would come along. Walking the
long way to the gallery down the long side of the
park instead of through it, avoiding the ungrammat-
ical commands mounted on the gates and paths, I
noticed people photographing themselves and others, asking myself how they knew when the right
moment for photographing was, even as I saw that
they were photographing in every moment, an accu-
mulated grabbing of time from the stream of life for
later sifting and labeling, a large net cast over time in
the hope of catching the right moment and keeping

it. There was a great deal of photographing going on along the long side of the park in that moment or every moment, the light was the best light to come along in every moment, a condition that I had not understood to be the case in my photographing the egg on the ledge near my desk in a sly manner.

What was the difference between the world and the photographed world was a question I was forced to ask myself often in the past, I recalled again as I walked to the gallery down the long side of the park, could there be said to be at any moment an absolute value of the world which a photograph would reveal, which anyone looking at the photograph would immediately see. Or was it possible that the photographed world would be revealed to be a joke-seeming world, the absolute value of the world thus being a joke. With people photographing all around me along the long side of the park, it was a question—the question of the absolute value of the world in a photograph—that was in the air, it was a question not beyond the pale for anyone photographing down the long side of the park, whether any of them considered the question in that moment or any moment was a question, an open question unanswerable without having access to every person's mentality always. If I photographed the egg would its mysteries or the mysteries of the world or the joke-seeming world be revealed, I had asked myself after some days or weeks of observing

the egg at my job and also while clinging to a subway pole, then asking myself whether photographing it not once but on subsequent days would leave
me able to observe or perceive any shift in its truth
and from the shift then deduce or remove a layer
of remove from the truth unburied. This being a
question of photographing as well as of knowing
the truth about any object. Would two days' photographing reveal something different from three
days' photographing, and four days', and so forth,
I had asked myself. If I photographed the egg every
day over time at whatever time was the right time,
would I, observing and perceiving it in front of me
and through the camera lens, understand or begin
to understand the difference between the world
and the photographed world, would the egg be a
constant around which I could test photography
as a tool, photography being inconstant, being as
it was subject to me, the person photographing,
and the light as it moved across the room. Every
morning first thing, as it turned out, I recalled as
I continued walking down the long side of the
park, in the preblemished morning light was the
best time for photographing the egg on the ledge
as well as for photographing various other objects
borrowed from the zone of my so-called studio and
the zone of various cupboards and drawers at my
job, one of them—the objects—being a pocket-size
cassette recorder found in the back of a drawer in

the spatiotemporal unknown and mystifying in its own right, nothing in my job requiring the use of a pocket-size cassette recorder, nothing in the moving of items into the "completed" column requiring the use of a pocket-size cassette recorder, my imagination being further insufficient for producing a scenario in which it would. I continued photographing the egg and the pocket-size cassette recorder and various other objects every morning on the ledge near my desk, continuing the project of photographing day after day even as I became less and less sure of what I was learning from it. For example, would the photographed world in the form of a photographed egg reveal the truth of the object or would it instead reveal whatever it was that patrolled the border of the realm of knowing the truth about anything.

Finishing walking down the long side of the park I considered the philosophical objects I had attempted making at my job at some point between other points, at some point when the categories *time, allotment of* and *finances, allotment of or rather lack thereof in the life of the artist* were under shall we say pressure. These objects or actions constituted my building architectural models using two kinds of tape, hacking erasers into bits and dust and covertly photographing the resultant piles of bits and dust, arranging the objects on my desk to resemble an abandoned city and photographing the resultant city. These objects and actions however had failed—hacking an eraser to bits not being, for one thing, as it was not, an efficacious manner of avoiding slant looks from my boss or anyone. Hacking an eraser to bits being a terrible double agent in this respect. Moreover they—the objects and actions—came into the world as dead objects rather than philosophical objects, they immediately became null things, which I later understood to be the result of beginning with the idea and not the material, I was thinking as I finished walking down the long side of the park. The deadness and nullity was the result of beginning with the idea of making my job my patron and then trying to do it, resultantly producing objects and actions dead on arrival, having come as they did out of the idea of dovetailing my job and my work, of dovetailing cultural production and labor at work under the conditions of late-capitalistic society, an idea I had found compelling but the resulting forms less so, I thought as I passed the corner of the park and prepared to reenter the grid. The objects had arrived dead and were even more dead post, seen later in my so-called studio, the context of my so-called studio bringing, as it did, it must be said, nothing to the table, so that I had produced not philosophical objects but merely philosophy. Even as it was impossible to imagine a philosophy for which a hacked-up eraser might be an object of consideration, unlike Descartes's wax, I had thought in confusion. Philosophy or meaning in the case of the hacked-up eraser, I later understood, should have come up from the materials, from being curious about your—my—materials and seeing what came out of them, knowing your—my—materials, deeply knowing them, discovering the ways in which they worked and the ways in which they didn't. In some art producing the woken-up feeling, this resembled or produced a feeling of materials guided inevitably but newly, in other art resembling something more like materials subdued and doing what they were not meant to do. Letting meaning come up from materials was a way of avoiding limiting what you were—I was—seeing or making or already assigning meaning, letting meaning come up also being a way of letting things lead to other things, like the sculptor Engman inventing a new kind of golf club with his insight into shape and movement and form. The guiding or subduing or both leading to feelings of waking up and spiking out into time in the—my—most gratifying encounters with objects or art, on first and subsequent encounters, not therefore producing feelings of merely illustrating an idea, merely illustrating being a quick path to the work going flat. Moreover I did not want to already know what my work meant, whatever my work was, I wanted to make it in order to find out what it meant, these two things being impossible to be simultaneously true no matter which path I took to try connecting them. This I felt to be deeply true, even as I knew that the opposite could be true, I had seen this to be true with artists who started with nothing more than an idea plus a typewriter and an action or two. Which is to say that I could not stop myself pursuing ideas and considering what their form should be, wanting as I did to see what they looked like.

Also contributing, I was thinking as I reentered the grid, to the deadness on arrival of the works made of stolen materials on stolen time was the appearance in various art galleries at that time of other artists' work made with office materials, whether stolen or made on stolen time being something unmentioned in the artist materials available to be read, even as I believed firmly at the time, a time between others, that work made in stolen materials on stolen time was the only kind of work possible in our late-capitalistic society, in which all or most of your—our— time is stolen. Studying however the objects made by others from office materials, source unknown, in art galleries on my lunch break, I considered not for the first time the ways in which I expected things to mean what I thought they should mean. Looking at works made from office supplies—mailing labels, pencil shavings, circle stickers in two sizes in neon colors, retired printer paper with sprocket holes along the side—I found myself asking what they in fact meant or revealed, being unable tell in that moment how much thought or real thought had gone into them or any art, my instinct for measuring or determining how much thought or real thought went into art being variable and depending on the frequency of my smoking breaks that morning and the way the light had moved across the room. Certainly some of the works made with office materials, source unknown, seemed to me to be gestures rather than objects of meaning, office materials presented in a place they weren't meant to be. Relying only on instinct and history, so far as I knew it, to determine what was art and what was gesture, or merely gesture, I asked myself what the works made from mailing labels meant or revealed. One of my favorite things said about art, said in fact, I thought, by Jasper Johns, I thought as I walked, was that you take something and do something to it and then do something else. This seeming true to me, very nearly an absolute value, it also however seemed true that sometimes just deploying a reasonable amount of real thought could be understood to constitute doing something, still often the deployment of a reasonable amount of real thought seemed missing from the art I saw in galleries on my lunch break or any additional odd moments of unstolen time, that the work made a gesture toward an idea or movement or moment from the history of philosophical objects and then stopped there, not being resultantly an object or a philosophy, that perhaps there should be two terms, *art* and *gesture* or *merely gesture*, for work that took something and did something to it but failed to do something else.

It being however in fact entirely possible that artwork I had consigned to the category *work, merely gesture* or the category *work, incomplete*—work in this case made of office products which to my mind had failed to flit from the category *office products, used in office* to category *office products, gratifying work made from*—was in fact gratifying work relating to the flitting or lurching of materials from one category to another made in materials whose purpose was to create categories and enforce them. It therefore was possible, in fact entirely possible, that these works were not null things but belonged to the category *work, sly and subversive*, a sly cascade of subversion going right over my head and causing me to enter a zone of not understanding what I was looking at or why. Here then was work flitting between grand sly gesture and unplumbed seriousness, here was my lunch break coming to an end and me walking back to my job, here then was my boss: glass door, office, slant.

Was borrowing objects from your—my—job something that constituted taking something, I considered at the time and now, in the grid with raise plow and the long side of the park behind me, having turned down a street of oddly specific shops. Having borrowed and taken them—the borrowed objects—home to photograph them in my so-called

studio to observe whether they would wither out
of context or, more precisely, the ways in which
they would wither, I thought in my more cynical
or confident moments, I then tracked them—the
observations—in a small old notebook, observing
the borrowed objects in the so-called annex of my
so-called studio, a.k.a. on the hideous quilt covering my bed, as well as again on the ledge near the
spatiotemporal unknown, this requiring the portaging daily of various objects and the notebook in my
backpack, portaging between the zones of office and
so-called studio, thus rendering the backpack heavy
and charged or fraught, resultantly causing neck pain
and difficulty remaining balanced in subways hurtling between stations. Keeping track of observable
qualities siphoned off to some degree my keyed-up
feelings about the numerous and variable truths of
various objects from one observation opportunity
to the next, even as those keyed-up feelings led me
to dictate my observations from the notebook as
dispatches into the pocket-size cassette recorder,
adopting for this task a Slavic-style accent, the dispatches resultantly seeming to arrive for me from
someone somewhere else. Perhaps this voice could
tell me what my work was, I had thought. The
accented voice eventually however becoming as it
did a kind of object, impossible as it was for me to
stop myself thinking about the object quality of the
accented voice or my approximation of it, a voice

not my own, thus something with qualities requiring observing and noting, I thus became worried about the infinite proliferation of things becoming objects to be observed, of things wanting observing and photographing endlessly into the future, of observations wanting noting, of photographs wanting observing and subsequent truths wanting noting and composing into dispatches for the pocket-size cassette recorder, all of it requiring the control and portioning out of the category *time, allotment of* to a nearly extreme degree, thus impeding my ability to plunge forward with the project of understanding the truth about any object and answering the question of what my work was. Not to mention the question of how to photograph an adopted Slavic-style accent. Shortcuts there almost certainly were, even as I found shortcuts unappealing and never considered taking them. A process achieved by shortcut was not in fact a process at all, could not be called a *process*, I thought then and subsequently, I recalled as I walked. I was not mad keen for shortcuts, I did not care for them at all.

There then was the question of what to do on days when the observing and noting and photographing couldn't be done, having arisen as it did—the question—on the morning of the train situation or one of many frequent a.m. train situations, of the abrupt stopping, flickering, clinging, eventual lurching into the station and the state of exhaustion in which I resultantly staggered into the office. Would I need some sort of a placeholder, I had asked myself as I staggered, I recalled as I walked, if I arrived too late for the half-hour of gearing up for my job, too late for the observing and photographing and noting in the half-hour before work when everyone was gearing up to do their jobs rather than doing their jobs. Further what effect would a placeholder have on the aggregate of observations, being as it would be a break, a hiccup, a void, an interference in the steady gathering of observations and truths about objects. There also being placeholders necessary after my boss had happened to ask me when I was planning on returning the pocket-size cassette recorder and one or two other items he had noticed missing, in light of which situation I was forced to describe to him in detail my project of observing and photographing the pocket-size cassette recorder and other objects in different contexts over time rather than being able to think further about placeholders. Oh, like the egg, he said. Not having mentioned the egg, I was thus in that moment forced to shuttle my photographing of it into the category *covert actions, noticed by boss* or the category *covert actions, not as sly as I imagined they were sly*. I could only conclude that the egg was more noticeable than the pocket-size cassette recorder and other items found in the back of drawers in the office, constituting as it did an object in a shall we say nonnative zone, although now shuttled into the category *object out of context, now noticed by boss* or the category *object out of context, settling into new context*. Not having time, as I did not, to think about whether I cared for this shuttling and possible settling—even as I quickly suspected I did not care for it, my boss looking at me, as I had anticipated, with a sort of slant—I had anticipated it and he had done it—I said I would certainly at once return the pocket-size cassette recorder and other items. This thus complicating the photographing, moreover the question of the placeholder had gone derailed and unconsidered, I recalled as I walked.

Even as I had found my boss unsurprised by my photographing of the egg and other objects on the ledge near my desk, even as I was frankly surprised by his unsurprise, I then registered that he must have seen many things much stranger than my observing and photographing over his years of bossing, he must have had many occasions to look at things or people with a sort of slant, unless the slant look was not brought to bear on anyone else, unless it was in fact a look, a slant look, reserved for me. What did he think about when he looked at these strange things, I thought, I recalled as I walked to the gallery.

On what was almost certainly that day or one very like it, having staggered in well post the half-hour of people gearing up to do their jobs, I had thought I had best get to work in an efficient

manner, leaving aside the observing, photographing, and recording, to say nothing of figuring out
what might take the place of the pocket-size cassette recorder, now returned to my boss. Although
I did not, an idea having arrived in that immediate moment, an idea of photographing the faces of
people doing nothing but thinking, appearing to be
doing nothing but in fact actually thinking, or even
looking at something, at art or their children or their
employees doing strange things or trying to find the
answer to any question, the idea presenting itself
in my cognitive space in that moment being not
showing the thing they were looking at but showing
just the faces doing the looking. In fact people did
not in my experience like to be seen doing nothing
but thinking or looking and deployed all sorts of
strategies, such as taking a smoking break, to avoid
being seen doing it. Indeed, it was a rare thing to
come upon a person doing nothing but thinking,
staring into space seeming to be not quite the thing.
How to photograph people thinking or looking at
their children without letting them know they were
being photographed thinking or looking was however a problem, their not knowing being an element
that would lend to the project a stalking feeling,
which was not what I intended, but their knowing
changing the quality of the face I wanted to see. I
wanted to see what they looked like. Again seeing
the limits of art and sociological experiment touch

and bend away, I asked myself whether they never met, had they already met, could they both always and never meet, could these lines be drawn. Could a drawing or chart show both taking place at once, would I want to see what such a chart looked like. Could a chart show me anything about a question of existence, could a chart in fact show me anything I wanted to know.

Why could I not see the shape of my thoughts, I thought subsequently and on my way to the gallery, why did I need a chart to do it for me.

The idea of the photographed faces having presented various or numerous difficulties and attractions, my cognitive apparatus gearing up to follow the difficulties and attractions hither and yon around my cognitive space, my mental maneuverings beginning to gain speed or perhaps already following and gaining, my boss however in that immediate moment gave me a look that could not be reasonably described even as merely slant. I therefore attempted buckling immediately down to moving some items into the "completed" column. A bored and resentful feeling having immediately presented itself, I reminded myself of Wallace Stevens coming into an insurance office every day of his life and also managing to find *time, allotment of in the life of the artist* to write poetry, whether he wrote poetry in his insurance office or elsewhere being something however I didn't happen to know, further I knew only one poem by Wallace Stevens, the one about the jar on the hill in Tennessee. A feeling of remorse then replaced the boredom and resentment, being as I was so deficient in the category *poetry, familiar* that I knew only one Wallace Stevens poem, a remorse so keen that even as I kept moving items into the "completed" column, I wanted nothing more than to run home and read some poetry, pitching the "completed" column to the side.

I attempted forcing myself not to think about the jar on the hill in Tennessee, still what was it after all but an object in a different context.

The poetry question continued dogging me on a day I had eaten a terrible sandwich or else a day very like it. Having attempted to spend the morning reasonably combining the requirements of the "completed" column with the requirements of my cognitive apparatus, I eventually was released into the unstolen duration of my lunch break. I had spent most of it—the break—on line at an overpriced sandwich shop and coffee counter, I recalled as I walked to the gallery and was suddenly hungry for an egg on a roll with plenty of salt. Whether the sandwich eventually procured at the expensive sandwich shop had been terrible because my cognitive space was dwelling on poetry or because the sandwich maker behind the counter found herself preoccupied with something urgent or bonkers or because the sandwich was fundamentally wrong in conception and execution I did not happen to know. But it was so, which is to say terrible. Looking for a table in the expensive sandwich shop at which to eat the cheese and exhausted vegetables on insufficient bread, I was surrounded by people staring with all seriousness into their laptop computers. I had considered, I recalled as I paused walking to the gallery and entered the deli with an egg on a roll on my mind, if this look of seriousness was the result of every one of them having answered the question of what their work was, not being able to imagine, as I could not, my face producing such a look. I was certain my face could only be generally producing a look of confusion or alarm, still I would never know what it looked like until someone else developed the project of photographing people doing nothing but thinking and didn't let me know I was being photographed doing nothing but thinking about the question of what my work was and considering what the answer might be. Heading eventually for an empty chair, I saw an excessively serious young man shopping for boots on his laptop computer, his serious look having been produced by shopping for boots on his laptop computer rather than figuring out what his work was, still it was possible he was doing research for a project about shopping or it was possible that his work was indeed shopping, how indeed would I know. Who was I to adopt a censorious air if some people felt, deeply felt, that the answer to

the question of what their work was was shopping,
if it then produced that look of seriousness.

Poetry being as it was an *oblique way of getting
at meaning*, as my friend the downtown professor
of visual and media studies would have said, it—
poetry—seemed related in a second-cousin manner
to the question of figuring out what my work was.
Thus was art one lens for looking at the world and
poetry another, I recalled thinking in the sandwich
shop as I entered the deli. But could you—I—look
at poetry through the lens of art, could you—I—
look at the lens of poetry through the lens of art,
did the layering of lenses produce extreme distor-
tion, flinging away meaning to a remote place, did
my habit of rarely lowering the art lens from my eye
have something to do with my not being able to
hold poetry in my cognitive space for longer than
it took my cognitive apparatus to fling it away.
Suddenly overcome with wanting to see if the excessively serious young man was still doing research for
his project about boots, I had nevertheless stayed
put, fizzing with wanting, having ceased trying to
eat my expensive so-called sandwich, I recalled as
I ordered an egg on a roll, even with chances being
ten to one that I was late for my gallery meeting.
Instead I had thought about photographing different camera lenses set on a hill in Tennessee, how
would I get to Tennessee, could I get a grant from
the exceedingly rare category *funds, allotted to artists*

for well-articulated projects. Maybe I could ask the serious young man which boots he had purchased and could I photograph them on a hill in Tennessee, even as I didn't know in that immediate moment whether I should take the young man to Tennessee, the young man seeming beside the point, the point however remaining as it did, as it ever did, obscure. But maybe, I thought as I consoled myself for not seeing the point and for my expensive inedible sandwich, if you can see the point you are no longer obliquely getting at meaning, you are no longer taking something and doing something to it and doing the correct last something else.

Despite my sandwich having deteriorated like the paper shredded into the category *defunct*, I felt no interest in photographing it on a hill in Tennessee, whether or not it withered in different zones or contexts or gained stature being in that moment an idea dead on arrival, it—the sandwich—had withered on its own, not needing me, as it did not, to do anything or anything else to it.

Walking back to my job from the overpriced sandwich shop on that day or one after it or like it, wanting to continue considering why some things withered in some contexts and not in others, my cognitive apparatus however took itself on a different walk, a sidetracked excursion toward and around its own tendencies and strategies for avoiding the pressing questions that presented themselves, with the avoiding, as it often did, leading to forgetting what it was I wanted to consider in the first place. Even as I attempted to not enter a zone of complete mental disengagement by using the strategy of walking the long way back to work, a way not entirely unknown but that I was not in the habit of walking, hoping to avoid the condition of not seeing what was in front of me, hoping instead to be alert to new conditions and contexts in the immediate moment or to things that required or might require my tender attention, still, walking, I began to imagine and could not stop myself imagining a map of unseeing, a map of places I had walked through or had a habit of walking through without seeing what was in front of me, a map of an invisible city or mental darkness. The question then being whether to render the map as any other map, as though mental darkness were a normal state. Which it in a sense often was. Should I show things as they were or as they were not, I considered as I took the long way, could it further be said that I walked around in a permanent condition of mental darkness. And if so, who would say it. Further I considered that my thoughts on different routes or streets were different, that different streets liberated or provoked or forced out different thoughts from the stream of life or deeply below, could a map then be keyed by the thought produced rather than by place, and could I then overlay all these maps on each other—a map of mental darkness, a map of digression, a map of streets keyed by thought—with the overlay producing a convergence or confluence on a single place of power or void of power, possibly. Possibly that place of confluence or void would turn out to be my job, a place that generated or drained all my energy for thinking about the question of what my work was, I had thought, I recalled. Would it be odd or interesting or ironic if my job turned out in fact to be the source of the energy for thinking about what my work was, despite the failure or withering of the strips of paper and the eraser hacked to bits, would I be surprised, being as I was, as I always was, prone to see my job as the thing that got in the way of my work rather than the source of it, would it anyway be another case of something fatally dull to look at, a null point, a waste. Critically my job needed to stay in the category *job*, without the enlightenment of subcategories, I felt, even as I had tried and failed to make my job my patron and had toyed with a brief period of wanting to know what other people at my job did about the forbidden category "pending," nevertheless I was in that immediate moment determined to hold on to the truth about this object, my job, and not let it jump categories or flit from one to the other and possibly back again, even as it threatened to be a confluence or void, even as I would not be easy with tolerating its being suspended between categories, deciding I would if necessary shoehorn or shove it back into the category *job*, even as I angrily felt it—my job—to not be worthy of a category but to be something entirely other.

Could I however pursue the truth about some things and ignore or create the truth about others, I considered as I resumed heading for the gallery and ate my egg on a roll with more or less enough salt without noticing it in any particular manner, or was this selective pursuit the beginning of a fascist ideology. There was always the danger of a fascist ideology appearing or creeping in, I had discovered some previous years before when trying to photograph scenes from an invented failed utopian community, staging and photographing scenes from a failed utopian community, the idea of utopia seeming to me to be the only possible subject for art at that time. I recognized the danger almost at once or recalled recognizing it as I walked and ate. Feeling then at that time in the past or recent past that art should point the way to a better world, whatever the work doing it turned out to be, I felt that everyone should be making work about utopia or talking about their work in terms of utopia or its relationship to utopia, my feeling that this was the only possible subject and that the artists ignoring it were wasting everyone's time being not however the only fascist aspect. Utopias themselves carried the possibility of a fascist ideology, there being the necessity of rules for achieving the kind of harmony that any utopia promised, there had to be rules for harmony that must inevitably however run counter to someone's deepest feelings, causing someone to doubt or feel different about it—the rules, the utopia—the rules thus reinforcing the feeling of fascist ideology for that person feeling contra, as that person's harmonic feelings turned contra. So while utopia seemed to point to the best and rightest alternative to the way categories in life in our late-capitalistic society were entrenching, sometimes terrifyingly so, they also pointed in the other direction, to idealistic systems that couldn't stop themselves entrenching and oppressing once anyone began feeling contra, the possibility or danger of fascist ideology thus creeping in. Having stalled or given up the project of staging and photographing an invented utopian community, paralyzed instead of charged by the ways in which it was pointing in both directions, still I could not stop myself continuing admiring utopian communities in the same way I admired the noncompliant objects and papers in the box near my bed, refusing as they did to submit or conform to any known or dominant system, whatever it was, annihilating the system by showing it up as useless or imbecilic or rather creating their own systems which contained categories into which they—the utopias—could be slipped. Or did the creation of a system into which noncompliant objects could be

slipped or incorporated point to some larger ineluctable system by which they were therefore encom-
passed, the larger ineluctable system being a system
only by virtue of its encompassing quality, its gathering of fatally unruly things. Or could it instead
be said that such a system was impossible, that the
noncompliant unruly things annihilated the system
before they could be slipped into it, the system thus
constituting a nonsense system. Was a nonsense
system still a system, I had asked myself. Could a
nonsense system be said to be political, did it point
the way to alternatives to systems that entrenched
and oppressed, that forced things into categories
they despised, did I then want the question of what
my work was, whatever it was, to encompass, I
could not stop myself considering, at least partly,
the political, if pointing the way to an alternative
to systems that entrenched and oppressed could be
said to be political, pointing the way to a better
world. Would pointing the way to a better world,
away from systems that entrenched and oppressed,
show an outline of the world by showing what it
was not, I had considered at a later point, would it
show the outline of the world in negative space or a
world silhouette. Was utopia the better world or was
fascism the silhouette, I found myself considering,
was utopia both the better world and the silhouette,
was all of art in a sense about utopia, pointing the
way to something not already being covered by the

entrenched rules of life, something in the "pending" category or suspended between categories entirely.

Even having taken the long way back to my job from the overpriced sandwich counter, I found myself having made the entirety of the trip in a zone of mental disengagement, in fact at the same time in and thinking about a zone of disengagement, a zone squared. Would zones of mental darkness squared be represented differently on the map of mental darkness, I considered, what indeed was darkness squared.

On my return to my job from my lunch break on that day between days, re-encompassed by the office and office time, I had been shocked, I recalled, to find on my desk a note from my boss, an irritable note on a torn-off yellow piece of paper, regarding my quite shoddy work of the morning, my attempting to combine the requirements of the "completed" column with the requirements of my cognitive apparatus having evidently failed. Burdened with the difficulties of the day, as I was— the mental darkness, the expensive so-called sandwich, the irritable note—I felt it then wise to dedicate myself to my job for the remainder of the day, to not make the shoddy morning into a shoddy day, thus to buckle down and move items into the "completed" column in a tidy and efficient manner for the day's remainder. Even as the question of what my work was continued to signal from a resentful corner of my cognitive space, I beat it back and thought completed, completed, completed. This— working efficiently while thinking completed, completed, completed—did not however have the effect of making my boss look at me with the opposite of a sort of slant, what the opposite of a slant was being an open question, my moving so many items while thinking completed, completed, completed being possibly somehow suspect. Was my performing so well, he was likely as not thinking, although who knew, the result of something suspect, of having for example drugged myself up during the lunch break instead of walking in mental darkness to the overpriced sandwich shop and in mental darkness squared on the way back.

Eventually, on a day after that long day like other days of thinking about what my work was, or one very like it, the view from the window near the spatiotemporal unknown began to impress itself on me. The city overlooked by the window and by me as I sat next to it, moving items into the "completed" column, I had eventually noticed, was a grid, gridded with office buildings across the street and in the next block and in the block beyond, I recalled as I headed for the gallery with my hunger having been shut up and a plan in place to be reserved and wary, to not give myself away as a person who could not answer the question of what her work was, in my meeting with the gallery person, the *gallerist*. Still I could not say the word. I had not been able stop myself noticing the city overlooked, the numerous buildings being grids layered on grids receding toward other grids and toward a vanishing point distantly flung, there further being grids of windows on the buildings set into city blocks, so that in odd moments between moving items into the "completed" column I looked up and out at these layers of grids, this causing me to think about the ways in which grids brought or imposed or suggested some order to all or most of the human life happening on the other side of the windows, any human life happening inside those offices and buildings having already been ordered by the orderliness of office tasks, of moving items into this or that column, the bringing of order thus triply or quadruply or nthly enacted by grids of tasks, windows, buildings, city blocks. I had eventually noticed when I looked up in further odd moments on further days the tip of a crane at the side of the window's frame, a crane participating in an unknown construction project, poking itself into the grid, poking in a stately slow manner, advancing slowly in on one side from beyond the window's frame, poking and advancing slowly in and out of the grid on the diagonal in stately slow motion. I noticed this in a compelled way, the crane's motion seeming to me as it did to be balletic and profound, diagonally slashing the triple or quadruple grid of blocks and buildings and windows and tasks in a manner that could only be called subversive or could only be called subversive by me. Even as with its profound slashing manner it was ten to one producing another gridded element to be slotted into the grid. My compelled way of watching or thinking about the crane prevented me from noticing my boss looking at me yet again with a sort of slant while I watched the crane ballet, although it had been a sympathetic, it must be said, sort of slant, I recalled while walking. Perhaps there had been pity involved. He had then asked in a sympathetic manner if my task of moving items into the "completed" column had been disrupted by something, perhaps by the move to the spatiotemporal unknown. I was fine, I blurted too quickly, at the spatiotemporal unknown, there had been no rupture, merely a momentary lapse. My boss having produced the appearance of being satisfied with this response and moved away in his deliberate manner, I asked myself whether there could be said to be any such thing as a long lapse, at the same time considering the likeness and unlikeness of the subversive movement of the crane ballet and the vectored slant look of my boss, both being kinds of diagonals, the one slashing the order imposed on ordinary human disorder, the other piercing momentary disorder and restoring me to my task of moving items into the "completed" column. I was aware as well of the crane advancing into my cognitive space with its slant movement, throwing a rogue bolt into my mental maneuverings and shunting them off to a tunnel previously unrepresented on the map. Could a slant both restore and rupture, was a slant a double agent announcing a shift, a double agent without loyal feelings for this or that. How could this be possible. Was the window in fact as well a double agent, being open to the possibility of such a shift, being as it was gridlike in nature but unpredictable in practice, allowing such things as slant cranes to appear. To whom was the slant loyal, I was forced to ask myself.

I wished momentarily then, considering the slant as an aloyal double agent, that I had invested myself in painting as the answer to the question of what my work was, in the long history of understanding or rendering space in painting and then obliterating it and killing painting again and again and again. Having seen and devoured the historical sequence of painters apprehending and reckoning with bodies in space, painters over centuries rendering first architecture and rooms that could not possibly contain bodies and then apprehending and penetrating perspective so that they—the bodies—perfectly could, a great leap forward which artists exploited or obliterated forever after. I wished in that immediate moment and perhaps a bit afterward that I was capable of rendering the grids and the rupturing crane so that anyone looking at it would understand the space and the rupture of it, of provoking or creating something like the first spike and vertigo I had felt seeing artists acknowledging and ignoring perspective in alternate paintings, rendering and rending, or rendering and rending in the same painting, the spike and vertigo remaining in the present day, available for me to call up at any time. Having heard or read somewhere at some point that the shock of seeing the first accurate rendering or depicting of space in the Italian Renaissance or elsewhere had caused viewers accustomed to the flatness to fall down in a dead faint in front of the painting from the shock of the flatness caving into depth—this shock being a condition of which my vertigo in front of the paintings was a possible variant—I could not however later locate or remember the source of this anecdote, still I chose to believe it, feeling it to be true in the way things are true without being historically true, slant true.

Still I was not in fact compelled by painting, even as I was tempted at times by the tools of painting—the vulturing easel, the nonchalant brushes—I was not compelled even by the possibility of an aloyal approach to long history or an aloyal approach even to the aloyal approach. I was not compelled by the act of painting, I was unable to force myself to be compelled by painting, painting not being, as it was not, a thing gratifying for my own personal cognitive apparatus in terms of taking something, doing something to it, doing something else. It did not create objects I felt to be philosophical objects, even as the possibility existed—I forced myself to admit—that I did not understand painting or where meaning resided in it, feeling as I did that painting's urgent questions had picked up and moved into the zone of photographing, which is to say that I did not understand the doing something else in painting, even as it was of course possible that the deficiency was not in the medium, not in painting, but in me. Whether I should dedicate myself to painting in order to overcome my deficiency or dedicate myself to something I already understood in order to more efficiently or quickly answer the question of what my work was, whatever it would be, out of any strengths I happened to have, being an open question. Should you do what is natural to you or what is entirely difficult. Should your work be that on which you alight logically and easily, or should you fight your way toward it. Should you—I—corral or discipline your disorderly cognitive apparatus or allow and even encourage its relentless maneuverings. Should you—I—bolt from my natural tendencies or run toward them.

What would bolting from my natural tendencies look like, I considered, having reasonably tolerated my regret at not having invested in painting. Would it constitute rejecting the questions that presented themselves to me again and again, the question of what my work was being of course an exception.

Possibly by making work about every other idea or topic I would make a hair space around them—the questions that presented themselves to me again and again—the answers to them, including and especially the question of what my work was, thus emerging from work that was not about them in a work silhouette. Which is to say, could I answer the question of what my work was by answering every other question. What all those questions were however was difficult to imagine, the only question I managed to imagine being to do with the primary exports of Argentina, this then producing the condition of not being able to stop myself imagining making work relating to the primary exports of Argentina, of finding it impossible to move on from the primary exports of Argentina to any other question. I could not stop myself imagining spending a lifetime on work relating to or drawing on the primary exports of Argentina, even as I cared precisely zero about the primary exports of Argentina, I could nevertheless see then how a person could spend a lifetime on work relating to the answer to that question, a lifetime resultantly not sufficing to create work relating to the answer to every question, a lifetime therefore not sufficing to force the answer to the question of what my work was to emerge in a work silhouette. In point of fact my work would then be relating to or pointing toward the primary exports of Argentina, the questions that would present themselves to me again and again would want seeing through the lens of the primary exports of Argentina, it perhaps being, that is to say, not possible to run in the other direction at all. How quickly I needed the answer to the question of what my work was being an open question—I knew it could not be immediate, still I did not want it to take something beyond a lifetime.

Thinking about the numerous and various points between immediately and more than a lifetime, watching the crane and tolerating my regret, I eventually or at some proximate time understood that painting was not in fact the right medium for describing the subversive quality of the slant crane among the office buildings, despite the compelling quality of the gridded shallow space—the flattening of reality, the flattening of disorderly human life into which the crane introduced sudden subversive depth or interruption. To say nothing of the strangled light beyond the vanishing point outside the room. Video was it, was the correct medium for trapping the slow balletic quality of the movement, the crane moving slantly in and out of the frame of the window, for trapping the piercing or interrupting of the window by the crane. Video also being, I recalled thinking as I walked, another grid element, being frames per second, being a row of twenty-four or thirty or sixty frames per second resembling a row of twenty-four or thirty or sixty windows. The frames thus being a temporal order further imposed on the disorderliness of ordinary human life. The movement was more compelling than the space, I had thought while sitting at the spatiotemporal unknown, even as it was the space that made the movement compelling. Why could I not understand the absolute value of compelling, I often asked myself. The space was the zone or the spatiotemporal unknown near the window was the zone, or could it be said, had I already said it, that the context was my cognitive space in which these mental maneuverings took place.

I immediately called my friend the well-known artist who set up situations, an action carried out on its own in an automatic manner, in the manner of the nerves of a rabbit running directly from its eyes to its feet, rabbits being unable survivalwise to spare a microsliver of a second for thoughts in the category *actions, carry out immediately or die* to be routed through the cognitive apparatus. In any case my friend the well-known artist would lend me video equipment, my unrouted thought was certain of it, and certainly—my cognitive apparatus kicking in here, taking over the unrouted action about which it had not been consulted, beginning its aboveground synaptic crackling—would demonstrate how to use it in a kind and helpful manner, not feeling, as he did not, that trying out a new medium constituted dicking around instead of sorting what my work was and doing it. Did my survival or my answering the question of what my work was depend on this unrouted underground moment, on this not sparing a microsliver of a second for routing through my cognitive apparatus, I considered as I listened to the mobile telephone of my friend the artist who set up situations ring, waiting for him to answer in his murmuring way, murmuring into his mobile telephone instead of speaking. It being necessary to act quickly, I had then registered, before the repairs being done in the vent were completed and the spatiotemporal unknown became a spatiotemporal certainty and I was moved away from it back to my usual desk unit, I asked him at once when he had answered if I could borrow some video equipment and quickly. Of course, he murmured in his self-contained manner.

In a secretive manner on a street corner that evening or one very like it, my friend the well-known artist who set up situations calmly passed me a small video camera suitable for hiding in among the wires and plugs that piled up around the spatiotemporal unknown, suitable for recording the movement of the crane as I moved items into the "completed" column as if nothing else were happening, the not knowing when or if the crane would appear thus creating a feeling of suspense, thus creating a feeling of the triple or quadruple grid being the usual condition and the crane's advancing being anarchic or

violating or thrilling. Having passed me the small
suitable video camera, my self-contained friend was
not however available or inclined to accompany me
slyly into my office and hide the camera with me
in a covert manner, even as I framed it as a kind of
undercover mission of making art via unauthorized
entry in stolen time.

Dragging myself thus home with the small suitable camera, my friend the well-known artist having
slipped off in his self-contained manner into the
lowering evening, murmuring into his mobile telephone, I photographed with my regular camera the
irritable torn-off note from my boss in the annex of
my so-called studio, against the background of the
hideous blanket on my bed, a nonnative zone, having already before leaving the office photographed
it against the background of the spatiotemporal
unknown, neatly cleared from my having spent the
afternoon moving items into the "completed" column in a tidy and efficient manner. In the context
of the annex of my so-called studio, a.k.a. my bed,
the note gave off an unpleasant aura of out-of-place-
ness, seeming both more and less irritable, or more
irritable but also pointlessly irritable, even as it had
been compelling enough to portage to my so-called
studio to examine in a different context. Lit from
the side by my studio lighting, a.k.a. a clamp light
attached to a ledge above the bed, the note did not
belong to but occupied the hideous blanket in a

stuck and stubborn manner. Could I make it belong
in this nonnative zone, I found myself considering,
did I want it to, could manners of occupying any
zone be changed or preserved through acts of will
beyond mere photographing or did they act independently, I considered again as I headed for the
gallery, the grit and tang of salt from the egg on a
roll on my lip, acting independently being as it was
an impediment or the only and greatest impediment
to discovering the truth about any object. Through a
photograph could I show or make people see a thing
not set in a network of things. Did the manner of
the object's occupying of any zone belong to the
object or to the person observing it, I considered as
I walked. Did the makeshift nature of my so-called
studio and everything in it produce or influence or
affect the manner of occupying, the makeshift nature
of my so-called studio and everything in it serving
double purposes of living and working, galling me
resultantly, living as I was among double agents,
being in fact myself in a way a double agent but
unable to say precisely why, but not galling me, as
it—the so-calledness—did not, sufficiently to make
me plunge blindly forward in allotting funds from
the category *funds, available but barely* for a separate studio unit. I suspected I would not be plunging blindly forward in the allotment of funds from
the category *funds, available but barely* until I had
answered the question of what my work was, even

as I knew I had to plunge blindly forward in order
to answer the question, even as it seemed nevertheless nonadvisable or nonsense to allot funds before
knowing what my needs would be. On my needs
I was all hither and yon. Supposing I landed, as an
answer to the question of what my work was, on
painting miniatures on the backs of spoons, supposing I landed on manipulating or welding large sheets
of metal. These examples having been plucked ran-
domly from the stream of life or thoughts, however
unlikely or doltish they—the examples—were, they
nevertheless, once grabbed, constituted an impediment to thinking of others. I was nevertheless in
the scrum of the immediate moment of considering
allotting funds from the category *funds, really quite
unavailable* to a separate studio unit unable to come
up with others. It being moreover in fact impossible
to plunge forward with the welding of large sheets
of metal in my then current so-called studio, making thus discovering whether my work was something requiring sheets of metal at all impossible, I
reconsidered. The studio question being one that
could not be banished from my cognitive space, signaling frantically as it did like a carousel that has
come around again, it was prone to present itself
in a pushy manner during visits to the studios of
artists I admired or happened to know, artists who
had discovered the answer to the question of what
their work was and were plunging forward with it.

Often when I visited I found them—these artists—
in the process of plunging forward although not
blindly, plunging with confidence into the terrifyingly undelimited world of possible ways to make
possible work, causing me to compare myself unfa-
vorably with them—the artists—as they occupied
their un-so-called studios and did their work.

Despite the dread and unfavorable comparisons,
I enjoyed visits to studios that were not so-called studios or did not give off an aura of so-calledness, the
specific tools of work—maps, chemicals, easels, camera lenses, hole punchers, lithography stones, choked
tubes of paint passed almost but not entirely into the
category *defunct*, bags of wool in the category *sweat-
ers, unraveled*, chainsaws, needles, chalk, lights, laths,
awls—there being of course further my friend the
well-known artist who set up situations, his materials consisting as they did of a laptop computer and
a mobile telephone. Via both of which—the laptop computer and the mobile telephone—he spent
days calling fabricators and functionaries and setting up situations, even as he was so self-contained
and streamlined he could work anywhere, anywhere
he worked constituting a studio or certainly not a
so-called studio, nevertheless he as well had a separate studio unit which he maintained in as neat and
minimal a fashion as everything else he handled,
including in some ways people. There was not a
personal photograph in his studio unit available to

be seen, even as there were personal photographs
mounted or tacked to the wall or discoverable in
piles of papers or vintage pornographic magazines
in the studios of other artists I knew or admired,
even as there were as well photographs mounted or
tacked to ledges near the desks of other people in
my office or my boss, even as I myself had tacked
up a few photographs of the failed utopian community, even as I rarely looked at them, not having
answered, as they had not, the question of what
my work was. I knew however it was nonadvisible
to too clearly announce at my job what you—I—
would rather be doing or thinking about than doing
the tasks of your job, your personal photographs
being permitted to boost your—my—day but not
to sour it with regret, you did not want to announce
that you would too keenly rather be somewhere else
with anyone else, even slopping about in the idea
of a failed utopian community. Nevertheless anyone
looking at my photographs of a staged utopian community brought down by fascist ideology could see
that I would rather be somewhere else, even as I did
not want to clearly announce that I was withering in
the context of my job and my stolen time. This not
being true in the studio units of artists I admired
for reasons including their time being unstolen, still
I knew the question of what kind of studio unit I
should consider allotting funds from the category
funds, limited and barely available for was a hedge,

that finding out the answer to the question of what my work was was not a matter of setting up the perfect environment and entering it but of plunging blindly forward in order to find out what environment it might need. Thus it was a *spatialized philosophical problem*, as my friend the downtown professor of media arts would likely as not have said, rather than being ontological or epistemological, meaning that what I should do was stop thinking ontologically or epistemologically and allot funds for a studio unit and continue making philosophical objects or discover what my work was.

Or would my studio unit in fact be a darkroom, being as I was often thrown back on the question of whether photography was in fact what my work was, being as I was interested in the difference between the world and the photographed world. My friend the British printmaker, impatient with my pursuit of the answer to the question of what my work was, said often flatly that I was dicking around and should pick a technique or medium and master it. Her flat tone and British accent startling and alarming me, still I understood that she used that tone for everything and was as likely to sound as flat or alarming about work she was devoted to as she was about what she was cooking for dinner for her young son, her husband having taken off with her young-seeming male assistant. The young-seeming male assistant had been learning or mastering

various techniques of printmaking with my friend
the printmaker in her studio unit, thus not dicking
around, not with that anyway. The category *tech-*
niques, mastery of was a topic that was sore or con-
fusing, being as it was a topic that seemed to me
spuriously or speciously related to the category *craft,*
difference between art and and *craft, used as hedge*
against the consideration of other things. Like the ideas
contained in the category *beauty, what is it,* the category *craft* set off all sorts of alarm bells. Was it a verb,
was it a noun, what was it really. Did I have a craft,
did my use of photography count or matter. Liking
photographing things as I did, being interested as
I was in the difference between the world and the
photographed world—even as it raised the possibility of the photographed world being a joke-seeming
world—I was not however bonkers for lenses and
the history of film formats and the chemical compo-
sitions of various papers as were so many artist-photographers I knew, thus not being bonkers about the
craft of photography but only about its status as a
tool. I saw that this called into question my seriousness, my so-called seriousness, that this made me
unserious in the eyes of those artist-photographers
I happened to know who were thus bonkers.

Obviously the photographed world would have
to include the filmed world, I reminded myself as I
headed for the gallery, no longer hungry but feeling
I had walked down this street a few minutes before,

its shops being oddly specific in an oddly familiar way. Setting up the small suitable video camera at the spatiotemporal unknown during the half-hour of gearing up for my job rather than doing my job, plugging it in in a discreet manner, I had hoped that no one at my job would notice my furtive covert actions, even as they were as discreet as I could possibly manage, I had hoped everyone was too absorbed in their own activities of the half-hour of gearing up for the tasks and difficulties of the day to notice me cramped and tangled in the space below the spatiotemporal unknown among wires leading everywhere. I considered however that possibly my activities set against all other activities taking place during the half-hour were not in fact all that strange, possibly cramped and tangled moments were part of the difficulties of the day for everyone else. Did the space below the spatiotemporal unknown resemble in any way my cognitive space was something I did not have time to consider, being as it was time to buckle down and move items into the "completed" column, not wanting, as I did not, to repeat the shoddy work of the morning before or on mornings not unlike it. My plan was for the video camera to film the scene seen from the window near the spatiotemporal unknown for all the hours I was at my job moving items into the "completed" column, thus creating a long span of the crane's subversive balletic activity between long stretches of nothing or nothing but the triple or quadruple grid of windows, humans, buildings, blocks. These long stretches would be called in the parlance of film *longueurs*, my downtown professor friend had told me, in among the longueurs I anticipated small but observable anarchic moments—an airplane's reflection dashing across a row of windows, the reflecting resembling stills from a film about an airplane within a film about a crane, clouds in wedgelike shapes, a stapler falling on the camera, my fingers making an occasionally exciting or brief appearance—even as I had yet to decide whether I should have the small suitable camera record at night as well. Would all those night hours—there not being in those hours, almost certainly by any logic, a crane making slow balletic passes in among the buildings of the grid—be wasted hours or would not including them violate the spirit of the work, even as I was avoiding predeciding the meaning of the video before I had seen even any results. Would the night hours in which there would almost certainly be no crane be an annoyance of longueurs or a relief. Or would the pouring of immediate moments into the camera be frequently or always interrupted by the significant overnight activities of the cleaning crew, the camera thus on occasion producing resultantly sixteen hours of footage of its own cord. Predeciding what was incidental and what was critical being however precisely what I was trying to avoid doing, I could not anyway make any decisions, I dithered, leaving the camera to record ongoingly as I dithered, knowing as I did that the only way to make these decisions was to frequently review the footage at the speed a viewer would watch it, fast-forwarding not being an option, fast-forwarding through the longueurs not being something that would tell me anything about what the work would feel like for any other person, fast-forwarding suggesting I was interested only in the content of the footage and not in its effect. Even as I did not know whether the video in its final form would be an hour long or two hundred hours long or a loop of as many hours as a person chose to view it, it being impossible in any case to make a video two hundred hours long if I were suddenly moved from the spatiotemporal unknown back to my usual desk unit, the video resultantly finding itself amputated and finished. I had to wait and see, to resist prediciding or talking about what it would likely as not look like or mean before I made it, thus avoiding losing interest in it before it was made, I thought as I moved things into the "completed" column, I recalled as I walked. This reminder to resist leading me, as it often did, to think about James Joyce in Zurich. Talking about something excessively before it was made could bring you—me—to the unexpected end of the process without ever having made anything, any object, all the decisions finding themselves resolved, the work finding itself dead on arrival, the work turning from a work into a dead work, a null thing. I knew that my having to recover from a philosophical object or anything turning into a null thing could take many days in which I could not bear to think about the question of what my work was, much less think about an answer.

How do you find out really what a work means, the truth about any art object, the truth that anyone looking at it would see, I considered as I slogged home after my job had ended for the day, having left the small suitable camera in place, hoping it was safe from the cleaning crew and their significant overnight tasks. Was it enough to know your materials, I considered for the eight millionth time. What in your work created the pull and dive and the spiking out in time that produced meaning in the most gratifying and woken-up encounters, held your brain in tension with your senses, spiked your mind for you back and into the future, sometimes moreover without your say-so, without being routed through your cognitive apparatus. Do artists chase meaning or does meaning chase artists seemed to me as I slogged to be not an irrelevant question.

Are other artists rinsed with regret was another nonirrelevant question, did other artists regret chasing or being chased when they should have instead done the other, did they ever, that is to say, regret the answer to the question of what their work was. Here I was brought around back to painting as I slogged, recalling some small paintings on wood panels which I remembered seeing and staring at in a fixed manner for some time on a trip of art looking with my friend the British printmaker. Disposed in a long row on a long gallery wall like frames of a film and going around the corner of the gallery wall onto another wall and then another, they contained, I saw, having first patrolled the row of paintings around the gallery and then having stared at them individually in a fixed manner for some time, rectangles disposed like blocks of texts, like rectangles in magazines containing or indicating headlines, advertisements, information or extracted words meant to hook and grab your attention from the hither and yon of the stream of life, or like some other output generated by our formidable engines of public relations, toward securing your—my—attention in the ways that the economic market shouted or insinuated or performed to get it. The disposition of blocklike shapes on the small paintings on panels suggested the text, being however as they were mostly dark or black—the shapes were black or night blue—they suggested at the same time or instead texts redacted like errors or covert information, like things that should not be looked at. The rectangles performed for your—my—attention and then made you— me—feel something like shame for attending. Or it seemed so to me. So it also seemed to me that the artist had done an interesting something else, despite my usual feeling that painting could not do it. Staring in fixed manner after patrolling the row of small paintings, I saw then that some of the rectangles wore a sliver or microsliver of color, a hair space of color, along one edge or another, other rectangles moreover were imperfectly painted in or over or were whited out or deleted or redacted and then further redacted, had been in fact subjected to all sorts of minor or subtle violence in the redacting of something you were not thus permitted to see. Another panel had a sad splash of rustlike color down its narrow stapled side, the splash constituting a sad escape or small triumph of paint liberation. How did the artist decide, I asked myself as I stared, to show a hair space of color here but not there, how did the artist decide to imperfectly white out and then further redact this rectangle but not that one, how did the artist decide that the sad splash of color should be sad and rustlike rather than sad aquamarine like a pool emptied out. How does the artist decide any one thing, sifting and sorting from the stream of life, plucking one thing from the stream and then not regretting all the possible others, were the circuits of the cognitive apparatus of this particular artist laid out like a surgeon's, confident in his cuts and redactions, confident in plunging forward toward this and this and not that. My friend the confrontational printmaker, her cognitive apparatus possibly or confidently circuited as well this way, strongly approved of them—the paintings—even as I looked at them and saw regret, even as I looked at work not my own and could not stop regret flooding or illuminating my cognitive space.

This vein of thinking while slogging—studios, video, regret—having over the course of the evening carried me away from the immediate moment, even after I arrived at my so-called studio, away from the things needing doing—dinner, the correct preparations for sleep—the vein being as it was not merely a vein but in fact a wedge doing what wedges do, opening up new veins for new torrents of new thinking. Thus I found myself awake at a late hour, lounging in my so-called studio inasmuch as you could call it lounging—*lounging* in my tiny so-called studio never being as comfortable as the word suggested, being more in the line of slouching in the space available—found myself torrenting along, so that what was required eventually was to drag myself out of the channel created by the wedge, the wedge having dragged the channel, and throw myself into bed like an undergraduate.

The wedge presented itself the following morning and many mornings like it during the first half-hour of the day at my job, gearing up as I was for the tasks of my job in a sleep-deprived manner as well as checking and switching on the small suitable video camera to begin its eight hours of recording the receding grid and the slant crane. There was a moment of tension when I considered that the crane might not show up at all, this question causing me briefly as it did to forget the wedge and the channel, still however when I sat down to move items into the "completed" column, there it was, the wedge, dragging, getting in the way of my job, opening compelling or alarming questions, whether the compelling was always in some sense alarming being another open question.

Stop thinking, I ordered myself.

The crane poked then into the grid.

Despite my sleep-deprived condition and my following these ideas down every ferret hole, I was managing the tasks of my job in a tidy or efficient manner, not precisely present in the immediate moment of my job but not precisely on a side-tracked excursion among my tendencies in mental darkness, a darkness that possibly should be represented not as a map but as a flow chart of one thing leading to another or some other form borrowed from the world of the corporate visual aid. But how would a chart show for example the immediate moment of waking up from mental darkness and perceiving what was precisely in front of me, of seeing the flame-stitch pattern in a rug or the sky smelling like a rag. In fact the fact of the small suitable video camera devouring the grid and crane—the fact that immediate moment after immediate moment of the crane and the grid were at the same time pouring into—being *captured by*, in the parlance of my friend the downtown professor and others, captured by and imprisoned in—the small video camera—made it possible for me to avoid looking out the window next to the spatiotemporal unknown, the small suitable camera doing the looking for me, leading me to consider, toward the end of the day, as I was continuing moving items into the "completed" column although perhaps a shade less efficiently than before, whether other aspects of my sidetracked or distracted self could be managed by small machines, could all the looped thoughts and alarm bells caused by a wedge dragging a channel or opening a vein of thinking be managed, could they be allowed simply to fall into some sort of recording apparatus without my having to hear or attend to them, to be reviewed later when it was convenient, when I was not trying to do the tasks of my job. But when would it be convenient, I was forced to ask myself, when would this review take place. Being as it was impossible for me to review the footage all at once, reviewing it all at once requiring me thus to skip the time allotted for sleeping, smoking, lounging as best I could in my so-called studio, considering the question of what my work was, the recording and saving and storing began thus to resemble the map that is as big as the thing it maps, a second life being required to help with the sifting and ordering but needing reviewing and sifting and ordering in itself. Where was the time do something and, more important, to do something else. Where was the second set of hours allotted to these tasks, I asked myself, was forced to ask.

As I walked to the gallery I recalled thinking, after a few hours of moving items into the "completed" column while immediate moment after immediate moment were pouring into the small suitable camera, that it was the doing something else that created the woken-up feeling of chasing meaning. The doing something else created the feeling of many things being possible, of endless connective signifying and deft ongoing correspondence. What often followed this lit-up or woken-up condition—the ideal situating of object in context or of context encompassing object—was that the feeling of context flew wide, the possibilities for signifying and corresponding opening in a capacious glorious manner, the context possibly being or becoming or being indeed as capacious as my cognitive space itself. Everything connected itself to work, my work, whatever it was, devouring the world through my work and all connecting with all.

Usually however the world was prone in that kind of moment to go flat. Which is to say that at the height and then downslope of the woken-up feeling, especially on days when it was too lit up, too woken up, in the context of my wide-flown connective cognitive space the zone flew too wide, leaving me then registering that in the wide-open zone almost anything could be or become an answer to anything else, even or especially an answer to the question of what my work was, a terrible answer, anything being an answer being the same as nothing being an answer, nothing being as capacious as everything, this being the condition that was prone to or did always cause my work and the world to go flat. Sometimes the world and my work, whatever it was, going flat being connected to other conditions, such as low blood sugar or having failed to sleep well the night before, ten to one it was connected instead to everything connecting to everything else, to a crackling synapse hiccupped and blown, to a work approaching and then coming too fully into its meaning. The moment a thing or an idea signified that all things could or did signify was the moment when the world went flat, when a thing came fully into its meaning, the lit-up feeling of endless connection staggering to the edge and then plummeting away. Everything being nothing, all roads thus closed off, the murderer revealed, the minor key resolved tritely to major. I could be looking at page after page of gallery advertisements in an art magazine or looking at artworks in one gallery space or gallery window after another and after another— many galleries being as they were located on a street with other galleries, those streets being located between other streets with other galleries, some of those galleries being situated on the ground floor of buildings filled on other floors with more galleries, filled from top to bottom with corridors of galleries—everything signifying capaciously, everything glorious and flying open and catapulting toward a lit-up feeling or peak of meaning, a place where or condition in which all questions would be resolved without rendering them pointless, then however the theme and variations—art being the theme and different artists' work being the variations—began to look like so much merchandise on display, like so much loot on display in the grid of galleries or pages, a glut, available to be selected through shopping-type activities, one thing meaning precisely as little as another, everything meaning shopping, the world and all the work resultantly going flat. A thing becoming a null thing causing the world to go flat, a thing coming fully into its meaning losing its power to mean further, a loss as devastating as anything I could muster or imagine. It being even possible that in certain situations all I had to do was say the word—*null*—to myself and the world would go flat. What did my face look like when the world went flat, I considered, what did my face look like when things went flat and intolerable. I did not think I wanted to see what that looked like, even as it might have been instructive to do.

Political work, most of it, much of it, the most fully political of it, I had thought on many occasions and when considering my disentrenching failed utopias, for me came immediately fully into its meaning, fully political work for me being something that made itself and the world, although not the political issue or problem, go flat. How could a person, I considered on eight million occasions and also on some occasions having spent a few hours moving items into the "completed" column, pull back from the moment before a thing came fully into its meaning, before it became a null thing. I could not stop myself considering the ways in which a person might chase meaning up to but not beyond that moment, up to the moment before the world went flat.

A night of real sleep, not the kind prefaced by throwing myself into bed like an undergraduate, was sometimes the answer to the problem of the world going flat, not however without leaving a resultant feeling of vertigo.

There was raise plow again, I noticed, registering that all my recalling, especially the recalling of the vertigo post the world going flat, had caused me to miss a turn or turn in a mistaken manner, causing me, I saw, to walk in a circle, having been walking to the gallery in a state of mental darkness. Would a serious artist or person have paid attention to the streets and what was in them and which street ran into which other, was it my fundamental unseriousness about medium and beauty and craft and the answer to the question of what my work was that rendered me unable to answer the open questions and walk to the gallery without finding myself lost. Was my fundamental unseriousness the cause of so many glitches I found myself in, I asked myself, not for the first time.

Certainly my seriousness or lack of seriousness had not appeared to bother my friend the well-known artist who set up situations, not feeling, as he did not appear to, that I was dicking around, this being moreover indicative of the variance of friendship or friendships.

Certainly, further, this—my seriousness or lack of it—had not constituted an impediment for my friend the well-known artist who set up situations feeling inclined to set in motion a meeting between me and the gallery owner or *gallerist*, a word I was working on saying, even as my friend the downtown professor of media arts refused to say it—my downtown friend often providing me with lingo which I could nevertheless usually not say—who wanted to know about my work, was interested in my work, whatever it was or turned out to be. He—my friend—had calmly told me this news about her—the gallery person—at a rooftop bar in the humidity. Drinking something with gin, I was brought up short by it—the news of the gallery person—it overcame me, overcome I could not immediately respond, my mind dropping as it was prone to do down a ferret hole of open-seeming questions. What did it—*interested*—mean, being as it was a word that could mean variously to different people in the same conversation, the range of ways to be interested being as it was as unreliable as it was variable. However could you know what a word meant, the absolute value of a word, without having access to every person's mentality always was an open question.

What on earth would we discuss, I had asked myself, what would be discussed. *Discussed* being a tricky word, my work, whatever it was, being as it was something that could be hacked away at, picked at, deliberately ignored, betrayed, temporarily annihilated, mindfucked to death, *discussed* however not being quite the thing. Was *discussed* a word that went into the category *word choice, different from mine* or *syntax, different from mine*, or was it a simple shift, something observable and dictatable into the pocket-size cassette recorder were I observing and dictating the changes in ways of answering the question of what my work was, a bottomless infinite falling through layers, at the same time a constant returning, an infinite something, an infinite loop.

We—the gallerist and I—further might through our lack of access to the absolute value of words find ourselves brought up short by each other, the meeting ten to one mattering to me certainly more than it mattered to her, a situation causing me to blurt out and torrent along with my thinking, causing me to try to square out loud what she saw with what I saw or was trying to say, an intolerable situation for both of us. What did this person, this gallery person, know or think looking at my work, whatever it was, seeing perhaps a shape in it or of it not yet apparent to me. I could not see how to ask her what it looked like, even as more than anything I wanted to see what it looked like, the possibilities for slipping between categories or meanings or misunderstanding feeling endless or endlessly open. What had this person been told or shown by my friend the artist who set up situations, had he *spatialized*, as my friend the downtown professor would have said, my work into a space or shape in which she—the gallerist—had taken an interest, there being always ever the possibility that our transaction could turn out to be a game of telephone, with the shape of my work, or indeed my cognitive space, mistranslated and changed by degrees of remove. Which could lead to her saying oh in an uninterested or even disinterested manner and me then walking away devastated and demented, a domino effect set in motion by the still-unknown description telephoned by my friend the well-known artist, a domino effect continuing dementedly ever after. I had not been able to stop myself imagining games, I recalled on the way to the gallery, on the rooftop drinking something with gin. All of this as-yet unblurted thinking having been in progress before I had so much as responded to the news from my friend the well-known artist, my friend smiling benignantly, stirring his drink of not-gin with a tiny straw.

I was worn out, I realized at the rooftop bar, *worn out* had become my organizing principle or lens. My cognitive space was in disarray, my worn-out and disarrayed condition leaving me prone to slipping between categories or unable to prevent myself slipping. I asked myself, not for the first time, as I sat with my friend the well-known artist who set up situations, what indeed my cognitive space looked like, new forms suggesting or hurling themselves at me even as we sat on the rooftop. Was it a place with numerous and variable signs and arrows and directions to other places. Was my mind like the jar on a hill in Tennessee, collecting ideas like a sound box or collecting or filtering device or lens. Were my cognitive apparatus and cognitive space the objects or the contexts, mind over matter being something the confrontational British printmaker liked to say, which was mind and which was matter being an open question, it all seeming as it did like mind to me. Considering the difference in my worn-out state between mind and matter when my mind was possibly both produced an eclipse or eclipsed feeling. Or was worn out the jar and I the wilderness around the hill in Tennessee, different in kind or category from the wilderness of the immediate moment, the conspicuously loud and young people around me at the rooftop bar.

Slipping between meanings being what it was in kind or category, I then asked my worn-out self whether this rooftop drinks appointment might be considered a situation set up by my friend the well-known artist who set up situations, a gallery person drawn from his vast and mysterious network introduced to his friend the artist who did not know what her work was, a situation set in motion in the humidity at a rooftop bar. Even were it not a situation strictly speaking, was it a situation anyway when set up by a friend who set up situations, which is to say that having identified his work as the setting up of situations could he do nothing that was not a situation, if that was what his work was. Were they in fact not unconnected zones. If all of his life was a situation, would then further all immediate moments of lives that touched his life be situations, would then all actions arising out of those immediate moments be situations. As the situations branched out nthly could all of life then in fact be considered a situation, I was toying with thinking, if all of my personal own life was thus a situation, possibly something constituting a part of the work of my friend the well-known artist who set up situations, what would be the line between life and situation I was ever crossing and crossing back, crossing and crossing back, the line I could not stop myself crossing as I tried to figure out the answer to the question of what my work was. This seeming like a dangerous immediate moment, related in a genome manner to the capacious flying wide that tended to lead to the world going flat. My calm friend, however, unconcerned seeming as he was about the world going flat, having possibly never been faced with a flat world, had sorted what was art and what was life, his work of setting up situations toyed with that distinction, transforming the gap between them into something less like a gap and more like a perforated screen, the image presenting itself being something resembling a screen in a confessional, densely and obscurely worked, gratifying to the mind and eye. Thinking of his work as a screen and mine as a line I could not stop myself crossing and recrossing into the future, another image presented itself in my cognitive space, the line bent into a silhouette of life, a life silhouette, being like life or informed by life or using the resources of life but not actually being life, thus revealing or suggesting what life was. Was there indeed in fact any gap existing between art and life if you spent your life thinking about art, if your so-called studio and your apartment were the same thing, was the gap, that is to say, the so-called.

Attempting pushing away the possibility of the world going flat, chasing my thought laboriously back, my friend the well-known artist sitting and watching me silently or benignantly, I was thinking that it was certainly in the gap between the real world, the unflattened world, and the world as chewed up by my mental maneuverings that any philosophical object I made existed or would exist, or rather did the chewing up of the real world by the mental maneuvering create that gap, the maneuvering making a silhouette of life, a ravaged, chewed silhouette. My friend's own mental maneuverings being likely as not performed in a calm and elegant manner producing a different kind of silhouette, elegant and allusive rather than ravaged and chewed, I could not stop myself imagining his mental maneuverings as a kind of murmur, a deferential murmur from a trusted source, *maneuvering* being perhaps not the appropriate word, suggesting something clattering and inefficient when what he received would be more like immaculate memoranda.

Worn out, slouching ever lower in my chair, I asked him what I should then do, what to do. You should call her, he said in his low pleasant voice. Whatever would come of it, I asked, his answer then disappearing into mental darkness.

Time having passed, my friend having said good-bye with affection and taken off in his immaculate manner into the lowering evening and his vast and mysterious network of resources, I found myself slouching in my so-called studio, thinking about the shape of things, whether the shape or silhouette of my work could be said to be an egg rather than a line crossed and recrossed, was it something else—a timeline, a solidus, a map—or further were we—was I—no longer in the zone of considering the shape of my work but now in that of considering the shape of my cognitive space, my cognitive space thus slyly routing or else not being able to prevent itself routing thoughts through my cognitive apparatus in shapes corresponding to itself. Its shape was however unclear, was it line or vessel or mode of transportation. Was my cognitive space a loop, a constant returning, or was my cognitive space a knot, or not a knot but a tangle, a tangle anchored by a spike which if pulled would allow the tangle instantly to resolve itself, bringing instant relief, the spike being obviously, unmistakably, it seemed to me, the answer to the question of what my work was.

Thinking about the spike and the shape of my cognitive space, slouching in the space available in my so-called studio, I was also listening to a fugue by Bach, having been told at some point in the past or recently that listening to Bach would organize my mental maneuverings. Bach, I had read or been told, would create or reinforce a mathematical order in my mental maneuverings without my having to attend to them and would thus siphon off some of the ferret holes in which I often found myself without remembering how I had got there. Was a ferret hole the shape of my cognitive space. Would the fugue bring relief, I had asked myself, from the spike driven through the tangle of my cognitive space, I recalled as I approached the gallery. This had not however been the case, having found, as I had, the fugue by Bach to be its own kind of mental maneuvering requiring my full attention, requiring me to attend fully, each thread of the fugue by Bach requiring as it did attention to the climbing and downsliding of notes, their patterns or inversions or temporal intervals, the many threads of theme and variation thus requiring as they did in the aggregate the sum total of my attention, my attention thus finding itself fully led or siphoned away from the question of what my work was, my cognitive apparatus thus in the service of the fugue instead of in the service of me. Moreover the fugue further troubled the fact or shape of my cognitive space, the relationship between the mental maneuverings and the cognitive space being, I was forced to admit, somewhat hazily conceived or lazy, one being as it was an activity and the other a location, like light being both particle and wave. Was the fugue by Bach particle or wave, I thought, I recalled as I approached the gallery. Did it colonize or haunt my cognitive space or did it hijack my mental maneuverings, taking them somewhere unscheduled or unforeseen or unrepresented on the map, was it— the fugue by Bach—an object, was it something to be described into the pocket-size cassette recorder in a Slavic-style accent, thus requiring my listening

to it daily, and further how indeed could it be photographed. Would I photograph the space I found
myself in while listening, would the fugue imprint
itself on the space or would the space amend the
fugue. Or was a fugue a map, could its relationship
to the category *time, passage of* be shown on a map,
thus requiring the inventing of a map for music, the
existing map for music, the notation or score, being
somehow not quite the thing. Would a map of a
fugue resemble or be a map of my mental maneuverings or would it be a schematic of my cognitive
space, I asked myself as I entered the gallery, would
I want to see what it looked like. I did want.

As I entered I reminded myself of my plan to
be reserved and wary and not blurt or torrent my
way through mental maneuverings and along ferret vectors, launching from stupidly small detail to
nonsense overall notion like a demented zoom lens.

The music playing as I entered the gallery was
not a fugue but someone singing blues in another
era with a plucked guitar for accompaniment as well
as the sound of an old record album's scratches to
go with it. The scratches evidently not being a problem for the gallerist working at the far side of the
room. Having had to give up listening to the fugue
by Bach the night before and other music on other
late nights like it, I was prone to not listen to music
while I attempted to make philosophical objects
or answer the question of what my work was, my

cognitive apparatus not being circuited, as it was not, to accommodate both. Whatever the shape of my cognitive space, it was crowded or dominated or imposed on by music, a loop or clash of loops. What was theme and variation but an idea presenting itself again and again. My friend the artist who set up situations was circuited to listen music often or all the time, mysterious electronic murmurings, his mental maneuverings being so sleek and self-contained they could withstand assault by music, his sensibility not being permeable by music or considerations of the economic market or any other thing he chose to keep at bay. Was the gallery person or gallerist so circuited, I asked myself as I entered the gallery, carrying my things in an old portfolio I had found in a junk shop, its busted straps making the carrying of it difficult but to me somehow necessarily so, in any case there I was.

Was it all an error, was this meeting or situation an error, I had thought as I had dressed myself that morning, even as I knew that compelling things had been built on errors or hallucination, I had reminded myself, such as the three-ships Christmas carol produced from a bout of ergot poisoning. Humming the three-ships Christmas carol, I had attempted to dress myself, attempting not to telegraph or signal anything about myself or my work, whatever I might think it was, with my choice of garments, including my indecision about what my work might be. Attempting not to predecide whether the meeting was an error, deciding that strongly attempting not to telegraph constituted a kind of telegraphing, I gave it—the not telegraphing—up, even as I felt signaling was still the more pathetic enterprise, more pathetic than strongly attempting to not telegraph, recalling and considering how often—on the subway platform or other places where people are or seem to display themselves—I was forced to think about the ways in which what people wore was intended to telegraph or signal or alarm or constitute a batsqueak or code, of what exactly, or, I was forced to ask myself, were people simply putting on garments they liked—another way of looking at it—was it only me who guessed everything and then the opposite, was it only me flinging meaning at objects merely doing their everyday jobs. Nevertheless I could not stop myself thinking about how people looked or how people made themselves look or how people felt about the mixture of accident and effort that produced however it was they did look. Did how people looked represent a clinging to or bolting from something handed over in childhood, were people aware of the clinging or bolting, what was the meaning anyway of an enormous leather satchel. What was the meaning of or truth about a beautiful enormous leather satchel or a pair of boots on a hill in Tennessee. What was the truth about an enormous new leather satchel carried by a not quite

young man of slight stature on the subway platform,
what was the truth about a satchel that dwarfed the
slightness of the not quite young man and made
him look like a child holding a bag for a parent. Did
the satchel signify, did it have the potential to signify
additionally or had it come fully into its meaning,
did it resemble or was it being called on to resemble an heirloom, an old-fashioned mail satchel, a
satchel called on for carrying meaningful things,
war declarations, last-minute coded communiqués,
relics along the pilgrimage road. The design of the
satchel being simple and modest, also old seeming
and important—but not as important as the things
being carried—was what it was meant with false
modesty to say or relay or convey. This seemed to
me the truth of the satchel, whether however it was
a universal truth being an open question, certainly a
plastic bag from the liquor store was also simple and
modest, asserting the same thing with no false modesty at all. The obviously new satchel of the slight
and not quite young man having as yet no history to
declare, its burnished copper color not having been
produced by decades of swinging against the flanks
of a horse or of being rubbed against the overcoated
shoulders it was carelessly strung over of a member
of the Czech resistance in winter but rather produced by an expensive dye applied at a workshop
or small pleasant factory, the satchel certainly being
a new expensive thing, it asserted something else,

in addition to its expensive price. Even as it—the satchel—was burnished, it gave off an aura of being new, still it looked new, even as it had been carefully burnished by someone paid to make it look otherwise. There were likely as not ways of fraudulently applying further creases or wear, of fraudulently implying decades of horse flanks or Czech shoulders in winter, such fraudulent applications being however evidently a bridge too far for the slight, virtuous, not quite young man, a bridge or border he declined to cross, thus accepting the uncreased burnished copper and the embarrassed expression he would continue to wear until it—the satchel—having acquired due to elements of the category *time, passage of* a suitable amount of wear and creasing and burnishing on his own flanks or shoulders, he would be capable of offhandedly or tacitly letting it be believed that the satchel had been in his family for generations, that he was descended, as far as would be understood by anyone watching him on the subway platform, from a Pony Express rider or a member of the Czech resistance, this pretending dignifying any other shortcoming—his slight stoop, his perpetually embarrassed air. The bag would materialize his virtue, by virtue of its aged air suggesting a self-contained person not needing gratifying or supplementing with objects from the economic market, unpersuadable by or impermeable to our endless mechanisms of advertising and public relations. Of course this was pure projection, this was projection in its most distilled form, any number of other things being possibly responsible for his embarrassment, such as the uncreased satchel having been presented to him for example by a lover after too few months together or any number of other non-bag-related reasons not limited to being stared at on the subway platform for an unusual length of time by me.

What was the air of a record album with fraudulently added scratching suggesting another technological era, I asked myself. What hole is filled by an object pretending to be from the past, I tended to think, does it fill it or in fact fill it badly, I had thought as I attempted to dress myself for my gallery meeting, I recalled as I entered the gallery. Did filling badly bestow the aura of pathos. Assuming at first that the aura of pathos had to do with the slight virtuous man having been caught in a pantomime or an indulgence, I later however understood that it had nothing to do with the satchel's expensive price, the same aura having been produced by a pair of ordinary quite inexpensive trousers on an otherwise ordinary young man wearing them while seeming unaware of the sticker tags declaring waist size thirty-two remaining in place down the side of a trouser leg. *A bought thing is a pathetic thing* was the phrase that presented itself to me at the time, a pathetic thing in the network of things.

Having entered a zone of slant sadness while looking at the stickers declaring waist size thirty-two,
it having seemed to me that in our late-capitalistic
society the only way we had to identify ourselves,
if we were not descended from a Czech resistance
fighter in winter, was to adorn ourselves with bought
things from the network of things, I could not nevertheless stop thinking about the telegraphing and
hole filling. Nevertheless there was a distinct aura
of pathos about the not quite young man's having
been caught in this indulgent act, this however being
another example of pure projection, most people in
fact seeming proud of their choices, many people,
the young and slender examples, displaying themselves on the subway platform inhabiting their garments as if their clever bodies had spontaneously
produced them, as if their garments had not simply been chosen and donned but were spontaneous
manifestations of some inherent cleverness. I resultantly aimed for my garments to say as little about
me as possible, not being, as I was not, easy with my
garments saying unauthorized things, I had thought
as I pulled on for my meeting an old corduroy skirt,
a T-shirt, some sneakers, even as the T-shirt had in
fact the name of a city on it which I had attempted
to paint over during a phase of erasing from my
garments any words. Hoping this didn't appear to
be some kind of statement, having already put it on
and being loath to take it off, I couldn't stop myself

imagining seeming to have the air or manner of someone who had considered changing garments in order to create a gratifying impression. I could not stop myself imagining changing and rechanging my garments, achieving after each change a different aura attributable not only to the garments I was wearing each time but also to how many different combinations of garments had preceded them. Was a garment a space you—I—inhabited, a space for mental maneuverings, I thought as I resigned myself to my corduroy skirt and half-painted T-shirt, did we inhabit our garments, I had asked myself, the way we inhabited a room or a building, was a garment a private or public space or was it a double agent connecting the two. I would not have authorized an aura of indecisive changing and rechanging for my gallery meeting, nevertheless they—the garments—would have given it off, I decided as I entered the gallery, having changed or rechanged out of my T-shirt and corduroy skirt I would have entered a zone of indecision, indecision would have been imprinted on me and my garments, ineradicable at least for the immediate moment, I thought as I identified the gallery person and introduced myself.

Slow down was the not the first thing but a subsequent thing she not unkindly said to me in her hoarse voice, hoarser even than it was via telephone, resultantly but it must be said only slightly taken aback as I launched into a torrent of open questions about bodies inhabiting garments or buildings. Most people, it had to be said, finding themselves willingly or unwillingly subjected to my torrents, found themselves unprepared, the torrents producing in them—the unwilling or willing listeners—expressions of shock or immediate exhaustion. What if I photographed the faces and expressions of shock or exhaustion, I had asked myself on several occasions. So much for my plan of avoiding blurting, I thought, even as I was torrenting along, evidently not having routed the plan sufficiently thoroughly through my cognitive apparatus. Still the hoarse gallerist did not, I was forced to admit, look shocked or exhausted as I did it—the torrenting—only slightly taken aback. Neither was she shocked or fazed by my philosophical objects as I brought them out one by one, propelling myself into descriptions of their various states of unfinish, heedlessly discarding my plan of being wary and reserved. We had spread out my work, such as it was, on a worktable in the back of the gallery, or rather we ordered my philosophical objects which I had slung from my busted-strapped portfolio out into the world. There were the pocket-size cassettes, color coded with adhesive office dots by object or observation or quality of the Slavic-style accent or the light moving across the room. The pocket-size cassette recorder, now on my boss's desk for use in some task I could not imagine, was not available to be seen, even as it had occurred to

me that there being no task for which it—the pocket-size cassette recorder—was obviously required, he
wanted merely to be sure I hadn't sold it for example
on the black market. There on my laptop were the
photographs of objects in different contexts, the egg
and other objects including the pocket-size cassette
recorder in different contexts, the pocket-size cassette recorder now back in the context of my boss's
hands instead of in the context of the black market.
Would my boss ever consent to my photographing
him holding the cassette recorder in his hands, his
face with whatever look, slant or otherwise, being
in or out of the frame, I considered, the slant look
almost in that case certainly giving over to a look
of utter bafflement. There on the worktable were
prints of my photographs of the failed staged utopian community, prefailure, before the appearance
of fascist ideology in my thinking. There were the
large drawings of diagrammed sentences of my own
syntax and the syntax of others, whether a drawing
of a diagram was a drawing or a diagram remaining
for me an open question. There being no material
evidence of the video of the balletic crane and its
slow anarchic movement, I was forced to describe it
in sentences of my own syntax, to which she listened
with every indication of interest.

What was she hearing as I described, I asked
myself, what was behind the look of every indication of interest.

The hoarse gallerist asked as she clicked how I saw the photographs of objects in different contexts. *Realize them* were in fact the words she used, how would we realize them, as my friend the downtown professor of media arts also would have said. Could I work with someone whose syntax was so different from mine, I asked myself, or would the objects dictate the syntax for both of us, was syntax subject to a previously unmapped fascist object quality, I asked myself. Attempting to use my mind's eye to consider the object status of the photographs of objects, the objects showing objects, to see them as for example objects on a gallery wall, I was instead gratified, I was forced to admit, by how whatever truth about any object the photographs revealed could be glimpsed only in an immediate moment as the hoarse gallerist clicked through, in a microsliver of a moment, the truth about any object being possibly a fleeting thing acted on by various and numerous variables, becoming a set of immediate moments in the aggregate, a rather rapid slide show thus bringing this truth about the truth about any object to bear on the photographs of objects in different contexts. Whether I was not able to think of anything but what was right in front of me—the hoarse gallerist clicking through—whether it was a good idea or I was merely suggestible was an open question. But would considerations of the economic market allow it, I considered, even as I knew it was difficult or

repellant, I said as I watched her clicking through,
for me to consider the economic market. Any gallerist concerned with the economic market would
have to be my remedial mind's eye in this regard. I
was not easy with it—a gallerist's functioning as my
mind's eye—I did not in fact care for it. So the photographs are nonobjects, the hoarse gallerist said.
No, I mean yes, I said, even as the term *nonobject*
was suspect, seeming to foreclose on other possibilities on which I was not prepared to foreclose.
She said she saw what I meant, my response having been nonobjectionable. Beset by an impulse to
say more, I then hesitated, even as I was aware that
hesitating on my part constituted a kind of dither-
ing, aware that in a worst-case scenario my dither-
ing opened a door that some unscrupulous person
might take the opportunity to walk through, thus
creating a situation in which some unscrupulous
person would walk through the door and exploit
my indecision, my work thus becoming the sum of
an unscrupulous person's ideas and not my own, my
work becoming a shell and I a shill.

No door having opened, I forced my mind's eye
to behave, telling the hoarse gallerist that if I were
to print the photographs of objects in different contexts, they would either be as large as wallpaper or
preposterously small, as small as a postage stamp,
they would either loudly announce or declaim or
else force viewers to come unwillingly close in order

to see them. Even as I suspected these gestures might be tired, the announcing and forcing. Both of them, too, having a feeling related in a faint manner, in a pen-pal manner, to fascist ideology. Both strategies could work, she said reasonably, the fact of her reasonable tone making me feel immediately two ways, as most things did, immediately making me feel a thing and its opposite, so that any immediate relief I resultantly felt on hearing the hoarse gallerist's reasonable or rational tone was immediately undone by the suspicion on my part that reasonableness or rationality was not something I wanted to bring to bear on my work, whatever it was, reasonable reasoning seeming to me as it did to be tied to or echoing of considerations of the economic market. Philosophical objects, whatever else I thought about them or did not yet know I thought, did not seem to me to be reasonable objects, reasonable objects partaking of business as usual not constituting, as they did not, to me, compelling objects—objects to which something had been done and then something else—but rather seeming to draw on both reason and its opposite, to exist in a suspended state, a reasonable object only becoming compelling when you applied unreason to it. Even as some viewers of art often had an immense affection for unreason which others found intolerable. I understood in the immediate moment that if I was determined to make unreasonable objects that reasonableness would constitute an impediment, even as I also however understood in the same or subsequent immediate moment that a failure to partake of or consider reasonableness might or would lead to the objects not being made at all. This possibly constituting an impediment of a higher order. My further following of this vein of thought was almost certainly ready to lead me to a point of paralysis at which my wanting to resist anything partaking of business as usual would also want to resist any kind of tolerance for the nonusual, to resist what people or viewers of art wanted or felt affection for, leading me to the conclusion—as it horribly and paradoxically did—of having to make reasonable or normal or business-as-usual objects. Which I was almost certain I could not tolerate. On yet another hand, discovering objects I could not tolerate would be gratifying, this thought leading to a second or third or nth level of resistance, to this escalating origami of mindfucking myself to death. Opting in the immediate moment not to mindfuck myself to death, I dragged myself back to the simultaneous immediate moment at the worktable with the hoarse gallerist, calling a halt to my ping-ponging between a thing and its opposite, letting the thing and its opposite—the reasonable tone applied to unreasonable objects—for the moment stand.

I fretted, I told her, about the possibility of my photographs of objects in different contexts veering into dullness or going flat, not believing, as I did not, that the truth about any object was or should be dull, then finding myself telling her about my former plan to understand the difference between jewelry and art, the hoarse gallerist continuing listening with every indication of interest, even as she continued clicking through the photographs of objects in different contexts. Having thought I understood the difference between jewelry and art, I said, I however saw that I had never really plumbed it, eventually understanding my failure to plumb at an exhibit of jewelry seen by accident. I had missed an exhibition I wanted to see by transposing the dates, the exhibit I wanted to see no longer being available to be seen, the exhibit being available to be seen constituting jewelry—chokers and pins and rings of angled metal bits angled against each other and against profound tangles of wire, asymmetrical outlines cantilevered in a surprising manner, looking like tiny sculptures of a Soviet revolutionary era cantilevered on chains and pins, looking less like jewelry than like tiny sculptures, moreover looking, it must be said, like the meeting of skin and jewelry would be something like intolerable, that they—the chokers and rings—would be horrible to wear. I immediately liked them. I immediately wanted to wear jewelry that would be horrible to wear. They— the chokers and rings—moreover seemed to me not quite to be jewelry, if a piece of jewelry was so

horrible to wear that it sat in a dish on a bureau day
in and day out, if you did not wear it day in and day
out did it remain jewelry or did it jump categories
into or toward something resembling the category
jewelry, not quite but what is it really. I then needed
to know what it was really. Still the cantilevered pins
and pendants were jewelry, the word *jewelry* being as
it was in the exhibition title. Still it occurred to me
to ask myself why so many words relating to jewelry had an air or whiff of violence to them: *chain,
pin, choker*. All the same I was not mad keen for the
category *wearable art* or the objects the economic
market tended to adore to slot into the category
wearable art, I did not care for it or them at all, I
said to the hoarse gallerist. She agreed it was a terrible term. Wearing something was not the same as
art, I said, adorning yourself with a bought thing
was not taking something, doing something to it,
doing something else, someone else has done all the
somethings, you have merely taken it and aligned it
with yourself, you have aligned the object with your
own clever self. The hoarse gallerist agreed it was
an awful term, she did agree. So if the act of wearing something made it non-art, I said, continuing,
if as a work approached and then was attached to
the body, it crossed a border and left the realm of
art, if our bodies were so polluting, could I then
detect and identify that border. My plan, formu-
lated as I looked at the tiny Soviet sculptures, was to

come up with tiny sculptures that people would not wear but carry, I would distribute them to people who would pop them in their pockets and not wear them but carry them around, people would not be sculpture viewers but sculpture carriers, they would be sculpture carriers instead of sculpture viewers, thus becoming field agents helping me discover the border of the realm. Not being bought objects, the carryaround sculptures would not be pathetic objects or worn objects, the point being having the carryaround sculpture within range of the body, in proximity to the body, attached to it but not worn by it, wearing seeming to be the point where the object crossed the border and left the realm, where the decorating or polluting began. Could I make objects that detected the border of the realm, could I make objects that were suspended between categories or would they float or slide without heed toward one category or the other. Would the body then at the same time it was polluting be a key to understanding the truth about any object or at least about these objects or some of these objects some of the time.

How on earth did this interesting project veer into dullness, the hoarse gallerist asked, pausing her clicking through of the photographs on my laptop computer.

I paused, my torrenting needing catching up with.

Because I had no idea what they should look like, I said, any form seeming as good as any other.

The idea existing in a state of thrill but the form not at all. They—the carryaround sculptures—were an idea but not a form. They moreover seemed somehow not to be art or adjacent to art or even merely related to shopping but to have crossed the border entirely into consumer desire even as I had conceived them as exactly the opposite, seeming to me as they would have been to be objects that people would want to pop in their pockets, they would have to be objects that people wanted, this forcing me as it thus did to consider and adapt to what kinds of objects people would consent to carrying around in the first place. Thus placing me in a zone adjacent to questions of marketing and our formidable engines of public relations. Thus being without format and sharing a zone with our formidable engines of public relations, the carryaround sculptures became null objects, going, as I had thought about them, resultantly flat.

Was the distinction between art and shopping less interesting than the distinction between art and jewelry, she asked, the hoarse gallerist asked. Is shopping not a subject for art, why is it not. Owing to there being something extremely off-putting about consumer desire, I eventually answered or said, it was somehow pathetic, a bought thing being a pathetic thing. Being seen wanting seeming somehow pathetic, wanting seeming pathetic. Further, I said, for some reason not limited to my being permeable to the states or feelings of others, I was not easy with the wanting of others, I became offput and uneasy when the wanting of others was revealed. This being the reason I thought, I said, that considerations of the economic market caused art to seem like so much loot for wanting on display. Does creating something someone wanted thus become a pathetic activity, the creating and the wanting thus both becoming pathetic. There is something off-putting about any desire, the only desire I did not find off-putting being my desire to know the answer to the question of what my work was. And even that.

I had blurted this last part, even as blurting my not knowing the answer to the question of what my work was was part of the plan of avoiding blurting.

The hoarse gallerist waited for me smoothly as I torrented miserably on. Was the desire for an idea off-putting, I was then forced to ask. You tell me, she said. In that immediate moment I could not have said. It was possible, I said, unsure however but beginning to torrent in the immediate moment of the idea, that likely as not an absolute value of longing existed, an absolute topology of longing, so that the object of longing ceased to matter. My friend the artist whose work was setting up situations seemed to want nothing or simply did not want, his relationship to wanting then existing inside this absolute value, wanting without doing anything about it. What was then the absolute value of art, what was its relationship to wanting, if a drawing or carryaround sculpture or any unreasonable object incited abstract ideational desire and fulfilled it in a consumer fashion was the desire then pathetic or unreasonable to begin with. Did unreasonable desires want unreasonable objects, was it then a fine thing to tap a person's unreasonable feeling and provide a totem of it. Or should some incited desires go unfulfilled, I torrented on, was it somehow interesting or fulfilling to leave a desire unfulfilled, such as loving or wanting a person you were not supposed to love or want.

So this absolute value, the hoarse gallerist said, having caught my syntax, is the truth about any desire, whatever desire.

It is, it was. Should the desire to know the answer—

The carryaround sculptures seemed not to be dull or flat, she said, interrupting, doing very much what my other projects did, she said. What was that, I stupidly asked. Your mathematics approach, she said. Making sense of x, she said, or solving for x, although slyly, sometimes pointing away from x altogether. She said this lightly, having it seemed to me uncaught my syntax, in what seemed to me to be an offhand manner. The light then moved across the room in an afternoon way.

Time having ruptured and passed, I somehow found myself at the top of the stairs leading down to the subway, a subway line I didn't recall choosing. I had somehow left the grid entirely, had left the gallerist and the gallery in mental and temporal darkness, coming to at the other end of the rupture at the top of the stairs. Why I had chosen this subway and not that, I asked myself, why had my cognitive apparatus gone underground with this reasoning and the passage of time.

Why could I not remember the close of the meeting with the hoarse gallerist, where had my cognitive apparatus stashed it, why was I was permitted to recall only that she had said she wanted to see me again soon, even as I could not determine what *soon* might mean. A siren geared up in the distance as I considered the question of what she had meant by *soon*, approaching as I was the category *time, differences in opinion about lengths of.* How could I figure out the truth about any object, I asked myself, when there were so many variables, when any word looked at with a sort of slant could mean one thing and then another, including the words *truth* and *object.*

I needed at least to understand *soon* in order to stop botching transitions, I told myself. I had botched the transition out of the gallery as I had botched so many other transitions among borders in time with its overlapping constituent parts, I told myself as I did not quite listen to the siren approaching, the siren continuing to find itself in traffic.

Continuing standing at the top of the stairs leading down to the subway, I became aware of the light,
no longer afternooning along but getting on for evening, as well as numerous and various people around
me pushing around me up and down the stairs to the
subway, many of them muttering angrily or angrily
letting me know in other theatrical ways that my
standing at the top of the stairs asking myself how I
had got there was inconveniencing them, letting me
know that standing at the top of the stairs considering the botching of transitions was not an appropriate activity for the top of the stairs when it was
getting on for evening, that my consideration of
categories of time and light and grids mattered to
them not at all. My considering having no value to
them except possibly as an absolute value of inconvenience, except possibly further as a convenient
object at which to direct their frustrations with any
difficulties of the day. I was botching their transition or multiple transitions from jobs to home,
from jobs to the street to the subway to the street
to home as I deployed this double-agent action of
convenience and inconvenience, the double agent
working against my interests and theirs, botching
our transitions in tandem. I had botched my transition from the gallery to the top of the stairs, now
I was botching the transition from above ground to
below and from below to above for strangers angrily
and theatrically muttering. It was just one botched

transition after another, I thought as I remained standing at the top of the stairs, the siren continuing wailing in a frustrated manner. If I could just stop botching the transitions from any place to any other place, I thought with regret, I might make some progress toward the answer to any question.

What was my mathematics approach, what had she meant by it, I thought as I walked away from the subway stairs, hauling my dead weight or carcass down the street toward another subway line in the direction of the frustrated siren. What was x, and why was I solving for it, the syntax and the proposition both being as they were entirely wrong. Why in any case did it fall to me to solve for x, furthermore I had no idea what x might be. Did I myself have to know what x was before I could solve for it, I thought as I hauled, the genus or species of x determining how I might solve for it, does solve for x encompass both naming x and solving for it, does it elide naming and solving. Was this an appealing elision or was it not, in the immediate moment it was not, I did not care for it, I could not however at that moment say why. If x was meaning, if x was work, could it not be said of any compelling art, art that did something and did the correct something else and produced the pull and dive and spike of chasing meaning in a gratifying manner but did not cause the world to go flat, that any compelling art solved for x. Was

x the compelling part, was x the push and spike of the viewer chasing meaning.

Was the x in the viewer and not in the object, I asked myself.

The siren, I then in that immediate moment understood, was not in the street but inside my carcass, inside my worn-out self. An alarm or klaxon or an echo was looping or ricocheting around my carcass or ribs, I had been listening all the while or time to the siren as if it had been in another neighborhood, it had not been in another neighborhood, it had been produced by me. Solve for x ricocheted around the echo vessel of my ribs, ricocheting, looping, alarming, I could not stop it.

I botched my way home and threw myself into bed like an undergraduate.

The next morning the klaxon geared up again, even as it seemed to be gearing in what could be said to be a worn-out manner. At my job, even as it—the klaxon—sounded, I geared up in a desultory way to move items into the "completed" column, not being able, as I was not, to bring myself to photograph anything on any ledge. Still I was not easier with my job than with my photographing, I was not easy with any action or condition on the morning after my so-called sick day and gallery meeting. The klaxon sounded in a manner that seemed worn down in a dismaying or resigned manner, suggesting a resigned feeling, suggesting I might become for the klaxon a permanent context, solve for x continuing to ricochet around my ribs, around my cognitive space, leaving me not easy with numerous and various things including moving items into the "completed" column.

The repairs on the vent, my boss then announced, bearing down on me out of nowhere in his deliberate manner, having been completed quickly and early, I could therefore move back to my previous desk unit at any time I liked. The spatiotemporal unknown being thus threatened with the known, I thus became immediately or at least headed toward overwrought, knowing immediately almost without having to route the thought through my cognitive apparatus that I would never finish the crane video, to say nothing of understanding solve for x, if I left the spatiotemporal unknown, the spatiotemporal unknown in that and other immediate moments being critical to the answering of the question in ways I could not explain. The klaxon having finished its worn-out gearing up and now shrieking almost merrily, I blurted that I would rather remain here—there—at the spatiotemporal unknown— even as, I thought as I blurted, remaining meant the loss of the spatiotemporal unknown, which would no longer be unknown—if it was all right with him. Even as I had managed to not blurt out loud the category part in an overwrought manner, still my boss presented me with a look of surprise, possibly understanding me to have flitted from the category *preferences, person who does not express in an urgent, blurted manner* to *preferences, person who does,* the category *preferences, person who does* perhaps being in his mind the gateway or fast track to the category *person, demanding and unmanageable.* With a sort of slant tempered by his sympathetic manner, or possibly pity, he said he would see if things could be arranged to my satisfaction. Then moving off in his deliberate slant manner.

Returning to attempting to move items into the "completed" column among the klaxon's merry shrieks, I considered the arrangement of things to my satisfaction, what was it to have things arranged to one's satisfaction, could I arrange things in my cognitive space to my satisfaction and what indeed would that look like, actual arranging in that immediate moment being in fact unthinkable in among the shrieking. A drawing or map or drawing of a diagram of a cognitive space arranged to my satisfaction could only look, I understood with a queasy feeling, like a solved equation or a grid in which every question was contained. Would I want to see what it would look like. I would not. Did I not however seek patterns, categories, truths, absolute values, apophenic indications, evidence. Were those not the kinds of things I had in fact pursued with my so-called mathematics approach before the merry klaxon had moved into my cognitive space and taken over. Solve for x obviously prompted something arranged to someone's satisfaction, the putting of like with like in order to eliminate constants, if they existed, and discover what was missing, an equation thus constituting something like an x silhouette in the shape of what the hoarse gallerist had called my mathematics approach. Would my work thus be an x silhouette, would my mathematics approach produce an x silhouette. Was that my work then, the putting of like with like or like with liked, an ongoing arranging of things to my satisfaction, no more than showing things as I wanted them to be, was that it, all of it, tapping a dully reasonable desire, pointing toward an arrangement system that entrenched me even as it pretended to do otherwise, causing me resultantly to be blind to what my work was, even as it had been so obvious to the hoarse gallerist, a mathematics approach, an infinite arranging, an infinite sequence of arranging and ongoing forgetting to be continued over the span of my dismally finite life, a way of biding time, that is to say, until the end of my dismally finite life.

And then in that immediate moment the world of course went flat, x being solved causing the world to go flat. Even as I suspected that it already had gone, that it had long gone flat. The world had disappeared into the "completed" column, everything having been arranged to my satisfaction, the open questions having closed themselves or been closed.

Once a question was no longer an open question, I thought, overwrought, once the question was a closed question, you could no longer do something and then do something else, anything you did was merely arranging or decorating or shopping or assembling data to be analyzed by our formidable engines of public relations, entertaining us until the end. *X*, it was obvious, was death, you—I—can never solve for death, death did all the solving, death made everything null.

In shock I sat back in my ergonomic desk chair and stared at the ceiling. Staring at the ceiling tiles above the spatiotemporal unknown, staring at the irregular harsh surface of the tiles, I considered the resultant nullity of this answer to the question of what my work was, that my work was nothing more than mere arrangement until death. Put that way, looked at with that sort of slant, it seemed a terrible answer to the question of what my work was, it was no wonder the world went flat. Staring at the ceiling tiles, one tile having been uncontained, having popped out of its lousy metal grid and not been popped properly back in, I relayed the bad news to myself, understanding in that immediate moment that even as it seemed distantly possible with the right sort of mental maneuverings to make the opposite seem to be true, I did not in that moment or possibly ever have the right sort of mental maneuverings, even moreover as I attempted engaging my reflexive activity of considering the opposite of any *thing* that presented its self to me, its nonsense opposite, I could only produce dismay. What in any case was the order of things. Staring at the tiles, the dismal klaxon shrieking merrily on, I was forced to admit that the hoarse gallerist's answer to the question of what my work was had upset me, her having caught my syntax too well had upset some *thing* in me or rerouted my veins of thinking in such a way that it led only to death. Further I was forced to admit that her answer to the question of what my work was was likely as not at least partly correct, that I merely arranged, that my work was mere arrangement, even if an arrangement palatable—or especially therefore her interest in my work, whatever it was—to the economic market and to loot on display. Staring at the tiles poorly contained by a grid of lousy dented metal laths, the one tile uncontained, I asked myself if I could still be said to be an artist of any kind. Was I an artist of any kind or was I a person with an office job looking at her life with a sort of slant.

Aware of my boss slanting around the office, I forced myself to sit forward in my ergonomic chair and continue moving items into the "completed" column, even as I was not really moving any items anywhere but rather attempting to trace back the trajectory or rut I had been forced into, the trajectory or rut having shunted me from the path of an artist to the path or nonpath or unpath of a person in an ergonomic chair looking at her life with a sort of slant. I had put my finger through something brittle or thin, an ungratifying botched transition between states, I had come fully into my meaning and put my finger through. I did not, needless to say, care for it. In fact I quietly keened. Pretending to move items into the "completed" column, I was in fact keening, longing for my former condition, when I had been chasing or approaching meaning without coming fully into it, when *x* was not on the horizon, when *x* was not death, solved, completed, closed.

The cleaning crew milling about as they were in a significant manner, solving our cleaning problems, signifying the end of the remainder of the day, knowing as I now did that my boss had finished slanting around and was gone, that everyone not constituting the cleaning crew was gone, I returned my stare to the popped-out ceiling tile and continued considering the trajectory from open to solved, from path to unpath to death, thinking moronically that if I could identify the misstep I could go back and undo it, was there no way to undo the misstep, was there no way to portage myself back to not having heard her say it, it now being knowledge or self-knowledge not undoable by any method I knew or any method I was willing to try.

It suddenly having become imperative that I

leave my office and be anywhere else, the ergonomic desk chair and popped ceiling tile, not to mention the merry klaxon, having become intolerable, the popped-out tile unbearable, I jumped up. The office had wrecked my habits of mind, I understood in the immediate moment, in a way new seeming but nevertheless unsurprising and, I was forced to admit, likely as not there all along. The presence of the "completed" column having created a trench into which my corpus of work, whatever it was, if it existed, was likely to disappear or already had. It was suddenly imperative to enter any other zone. I grabbed my bag and my ugly jacket and vaulted or flung myself out of the office, I flung myself into the elevator and out of the building, I flung myself out onto the street. It was utterly imperative that I leave the grid of the ceiling tiles and the fascist "completed" trench into which my work or the meaning of my work had disappeared. I flung myself onto the street without thinking about where to go, thinking seeming beside the point, the point seeming to be only going. I could not stop myself imagining a voice shouting go, even as it shouted in a bored fashion in among the klaxon shrieks, continuing to be bored as I ran through the streets like a lunatic, even the bored-seeming voice seeming to have decided that the world had gone flat and there was nothing to be done about it.

As I ran, my job shoes smacking and clattering

over metal doors and grates, I could not stop myself listening to my mental maneuverings looping or spinning in place around the moment of the misstep, the misstep of having heard her say it, the moment the open questions had been closed. I knew the misstep could not be undone, nevertheless my mental maneuverings continued spinning or trying to undo it. My mental maneuverings were going berserk. A small different part of my cognitive apparatus, a different shape, a still shape, at the same time coolly observed the berserk attempts at undoing, one part of the apparatus observing the other, one part trying to undo what the other knew could not be undone, still the spinning thing was the dominant thing, the spinning like a carousel whipping me around in a more dangerous sort of ride. My mental maneuverings normally prevailingly being notions that hurled themselves ongoingly at me, the maneuvering and hurling being movement I could tolerate, what I could not however bear or tolerate was the spinning in place, it was intolerable. Was a part of me about to split off and take up residence somewhere on its own, I asked myself as I raced through the streets like a lunatic, racing in a straight line in mental darkness without seeing for blocks and hours. I was a lunatic for miles. I was a lunatic in a straight line, the idea of a straight line or destination—even with the presence or dominance of the useless-seeming spinning—seeming predecided now that I was condemned, as I was, to solving for *x*.

Thus condemned, I tripped over an invisible thing on the clattering sidewalk, causing in that immediate moment the word *fugue* to burst into my cognitive space as I recovered and resumed luna-ticking along, the word *fugue* dodging as it then did the whirring and spinning mechanisms, presenting itself in among them time and again like a light blinking on and off. Dodging as I was other people, occupying as they were the sidewalks in the way of my raced line in an infuriating obstructive manner, crossing the street in front of me in an infuriating manner, I asked myself in my demented state why *fugue*, why had my cognitive apparatus produced the word *fugue*, had my cognitive apparatus made a little leap to refugee, fleeing as I was my office and the "completed" column, or was I in fact in a fugue state, a state like an unexitable loop, a mental loop, an infinite nauseating loop. I wished I could invoke mental silence, I wished I could exit the mental maneuverings spinning uselessly and dementedly around the misstep, I wished, that is to say, that I could exit the fugue loop.

Time having passed, I found myself gasping on a street corner downtown, having raced like a lunatic downtown, gasping downtown in a noncommittal shape of light thrown down by a streetlamp, no lon-ger lunaticking along but with mental maneuverings nevertheless continuing spinning dementedly, spiking off now and again to death. I found my body could not be mobilized, there in a state of mild paralysis in the noncommittal light, crouching against a damp wall next to a pipe coming out of it. My body, limp and exhausted from racing in a demented manner, had had enough of being arranged or borne down upon by my overbearing cognitive apparatus, having been forced to race for miles smacking and clattering over metal grates, it did not care for it evidently, it did not care for it one bit. My cognitive space being as it apparently was contested space, my body as well was split against me, resisting or revolting, my body had staged a revolution of doing nothing, of acting out a condition of being unfree. Still in doing nothing I was chaotic, I was both null and chaotic.

There and alone in the thrown-down light, my permeable edges flickering dangerously, I felt myself in danger of invisibility, of crossing a border I could not cross back.

How was it possible that I could find myself both null and chaotic, I asked myself as I crouched against the damp wall, how was it ever possible. The null feeling was the feeling of being overordered, I understood, I had been overordered into a category, overarranged, slid onto a list of listable things. Where was the double-agent slant look when I needed it, where was it when one—I—needed to be restored or mobilized or else ordered into not caring anymore, even as I could not bring myself to imagine not caring anymore, I could not imagine accepting being not an artist but a person looking at her life with a sort of slant. I was or had become the grid, I thought, the grid was the null thing, x solved was a grid, the open question of what my work was had been closed by a grid, by death which did all the solving. Even as I could not imagine myself ordered into not caring anymore, I could not stop wishing to ride the slant look out of there, back to a point where, the misstep not being undoable, as part of my cognitive apparatus had been forced to admit, still I would be able to move my limbs again. The grid and the crane had been a formal question, a *spatialized question* as my friend the professor of media arts would have said, now it was something else, a botched grid metaphor taking up residence in or colonizing my cognitive space. Physicalized, spatialized, it had taken over, it had fascist tendencies I had not at first perceived, filling the available space and confining my mental maneuvering now to not only spinning but to pinging helplessly from one corner to another.

Not wanting, as I did not, to be saved by a metaphor with fascist tendencies, I was forced to ask myself whether I wanted in fact to be saved at all. Was the metaphor of the grid and the crane the only game in town, I asked myself. Did I have to come down on one side or the other, I asked myself, even as it could have been that the choice between the grid and the crane—order and chaos, category and noncategory, nullity and chaos—was a false choice, was I being distracted from something more important by this false choice and by the quality of the light stuttering on the sidewalk. I was not mad keen for it—the metaphor, the choice, the arranging of things to my satisfaction—I did not care for it at all. Why were my mental maneuverings so bound and constrained, why was I so bound and unfree, the number and variety of ways of being unfree continuing astonishing me as I crouched and continued apprehending them.

Bound and unfree and gasping I eventually found myself attempting to focus on a blinking light seeming to resolve itself but sliding back into mere blinking as I crouched and gasped, finally then resolving itself into a malfunctioning neon sign for a bar establishment as I crouched there, a malfunction turning the sign from *bar* to *b r* and back again, functioning and malfunctioning in what was certainly an infinite loop. Gradually the infinite loop of the malfunctioning sign—of *bar* to *b r* and back again—siphoned off the infinite or fugue loop of my spinning maneuverings, bracketing off a clearing in my cognitive space, undoing to some degree the body's revolting paralysis, allowing me to stop myself heading further, if it was possible to head further, toward overwrought and to take note of my surroundings. In the bracketed space a memory appeared of the disciplined confrontational printmaker describing this sign to me or one like it, describing and complaining about the malfunctioning sign, complaining but also admiring the refusal of the *a* to fully do what was required of it, namely keeping *bar* from becoming *b r.* She admired the noncompliant *a*, even as the malfunctioning sign, in a direct line with her bedroom, produced formidable migraine headaches, having given her as it did the idea for a series of prints relating to migraines and the refusal to function, a functionality silhouette. It was indeed that sign. Overwrought and unfree I had raced like a lunatic to the site of the blunt printmaker's apartment, being as it was only her apartment, her studio unit being free of so-calledness separately and elsewhere. Compelled by the malfunctioning sign I recalled the prints and asked myself also if what I was doing—racing like a lunatic while spinning in place, staring at a malfunctioning sign—constituted or would constitute to the mind of the confrontational printmaker dicking around, would I in fact know the opposite of dicking around if I saw or managed to do it. From inside my bracket of being able to take note I then noticed an oddly specific shop and then unsurprisingly next to it the liberating pipe and raise plow. I had run like a lunatic through the grid of the city to a known place, to two known places I hadn't understood were connected. Continuing to gasp in the thrown-down light I was compelled by the sign even as I was also compelled by my slavishness to the grid. I felt insubstantial, my permeable edges flickering, I felt like a thing unable to have any effect on any surroundings, in the grid or anywhere, I was a thing gone flat, a null thing, null and somehow impossibly also chaotic, neither *bar* nor *b r*, I was the botched transition between one and the other.

A window above me opened. I heard it and then saw then the head of the confrontational printmaker thrust outside. Looking around and down she saw me in the noncommittal shape of light. What are you doing there, she asked in her abrupt and direct but not unkind way. She asked me directly, not going in, as she did not, for loops of conversation, for fugue loops going nowhere or not progressing. A conversation about the question of what my work was could only in that immediate moment be an unexitable loop. Unable to speak I stared up. She then said wait, I'll come down. I then heard a child's voice complaining mildly or sleepily and her voice responding, blunt but gentle. Her head was pulled in, later the front door opened and there she was, carrying her small son asleep on her shoulder. Had I conjured her, I considered dementedly, with her small son sleeping, throwing his head back and opening his mouth to the moon. Had the visit to the gallerist and subsequent solving of x opened a rift in things that allowed me to conjure a blunt British printmaker and a sleeping boy. Hoisting myself up from my crouch against the damp wall, I then fell hard back down on her damp stoop, I fell hard and then sat limply, causing her eyebrows to go up. She asked me how I found myself. Without edges, I gasped. Spinning in place, I thought. Blurting then before thinking I asked was I serious, do you consider me serious, was my fundamental unseriousness constituting an obstacle to answering the question of what my work was. Back up, she said, sitting down next to me on the stoop, resettling her son. I backed up mentally, mentally trying to put my mental maneuverings in reverse. Backing up mentally I said nothing for a long time, or else it was a long-seeming time, the blunt British printmaker not seeming, like my calm friend the well-known artist who set up situations, to mind my saying nothing, even as I imagined that the spinning inside my permeable edges must be available to anyone who wanted to see it or help themselves to it.

· Having reached a point eventually in my mental maneuverings where maneuvering was no longer possible, having then run out of maneuvering space and been backed into a corner or up against a damp wall, I blurted again, found myself blurting, how did she know what her work was. I asked how had she gone about finding out what her work was and then how did she know when she found it. Why do you ask, she asked. I described or explained about solving for x and being solved by death before I found out what my work was. Oh, death, well, she said with knowledge. I torrented on, describing the crane and the grid, asking if she thought order was more important or chaos, if the grid hogtied the chaos or did the chaos pollute the grid. She then said, wait, so the slant is disorder. Not always, I said, sometimes it ruptures disorder back into order. The slant then, she said, going with me there, is a kind of freedom. Oh, I said. If so, she said, it's up to you. Unfree as I was I said oh, miserably. If so sometimes it is one thing and sometimes it is the other, she went on directly, no one is going to stop you from choosing the wrong one, she said. You've landed on a serious question, she then said after a few minutes or moments more, the answers are serious and absurd, she said, and hilarious and also terrifying.

Are you terrified, I asked her. She said I am, in my way. My work leads me toward it and then out of it again. She was silent for a while, and I watched her doing nothing but thinking. I found my work, she said, I tried different things, someone taught me printmaking, and I liked it, just as simple as that, I liked making prints, I liked the repetition and also the uncertainty, the theme and the variations. It was making prints that made me feel free.

Bound and unfree feeling I asked what does free

feel like, it seemed to me, I told her, that it would feel like plunging, although I myself am terrified of plunging. If only I knew what my work was, there would be limits and I could move within the limits, plunge within limits. Like once you know what your work is, I said, you can test the edges. She looked at me through the dark with something like surprise. Yes, she said, that was a fine way of putting it, I start with what I think is a firm idea and then work on every variation, when I run out of variations I move the firm idea slightly to one side or to the other side, she said, and then she started again. She was finding, I thought as I listened to her on the stoop, the infinite variations inside an atom, crossing limits or borders at will, creating a bracket of work and cognitive space that felt both bound and free. Do you regret, I asked, did she regret the work that went unmade when she chose one thing from many. She responded that she did not, she felt thrilled, I feel thrilled by all the things there are left to do and for other people to do, it renews, it stays present and urgent. Inside the firm idea all things are possible.

Pausing, her son murmuring and repositioning and attempting arranging himself to his satisfaction on her shoulder, she then said you asked if you're serious, you are in fact serious, or you wouldn't be here on my stoop in the middle of the night. I dick around, I said. You think I dick around. I was wrong, she said, she had not recognized the different shape of my pursuit, she said, she had assumed that the direct line and forking-off of her own pursuit, pursuing repetition and variations, would be the shape of my own. I was wrong, she said, you don't dick around. Your shape is something else.

Surely I knew that already, I said. Surely you did, she said.

So in fact I've learned nothing, I said. Maybe not, she said, but you've learned it thoroughly.

Her son continuing repositioning on her shoulder she then said with her abruptness but not unkindness, I had better take him up, and she did.

Continuing sitting on the damp stoop near raise plow, I considered the shape of her pursuit and mine, even as I expected the overwrought feeling to sluice back into my cognitive space. It in fact did not, it did not sluice. The chaotic and the klaxon remained post the conversation with my direct British friend, but softer, with their presences removed from me as if by scrim. The feeling was different, tense, held in tension by my mental maneuvering and my cognitive apparatus being compelled by the neon light as it was, it ongoingly was. The loop, the infinite loop of *bar* to *b r* and back again, the loop of my friend's migraine prints describing an infinite loop and the way out of it without, it seemed, the world going flat, the loop bringing the beginning of the direct line around to meet its end, this meeting not in fact closing the loop but continuing closing the loop ongoingly through meeting after meeting.

The loop was not a spinning circle, I then understood, overrunning as it did the circle, overriding it, a continuous shape, unfixed. The loop was a double agent, pretending to be a shape but being in fact also a temporal condition, a spiral, a spiraling vectorial movement of mental maneuvering, doing something else and something else and something else again. Order and chaos slyly mutually cooperated in the double agenting of the loop, the sly loop allowing them to slip borders and slip back again, ongoingly ongoingly but not the same, like the fugue, like the shape and temporal condition at once, both particle and wave. The loop being a change mechanism such that every time you—I— came back around to the top of it, words had different meanings or meant differently. The loop slyly pretending to be unfree but in fact being free, a spiral, an endless getting back. There were harmonics but not harmony, I now understood, having mistaken as I had the one for the other. The sly mutual cooperation of order and chaos was not the same each time, ongoingly ongoingly it was a negotiation, not with balance and moderation but with revelation and scorching earth, not with singing but with forcing, cheating, thwarting, keeping the world from going flat.

Further, I thought as I got up from the damp

stoop and began walking, further I had been wrong
about the chaos and the grid, they were not the only
game in town. They had their tasks or schemes, the
grid keeping the chaos from becoming an impediment, the chaos keeping the world from going flat.
Further the slant was the sharpest narrowest knife-
like wedge carving out from the glorious chaotic
stream of life, the sharpest narrowest wedge of one
color rather than another representing rather than
delimiting a rich or generative vein of woken-up
feeling, the regret I had assigned to the wedge of
color I now understood to be something nonnative
to the wedge but rather airlifted in by me. The slant
was not the same for any artist, the shape was not
the same for any artist, I now saw as I walked away
from the stoop near raise plow. There was what it was
for my printmaker friend, there was what it was for
my friend the artist who set up situations—it being
for him the abundant network of things that in our
infinite universe might ongoingly happen inside the
situations he set up, his maximal operatic situations
slyly ordered up to a point and then slyly let go,
things thus bursting or radiating out of them that
you did not expect or that he did not intend or that
he slyly intended but you had to discover for yourself by intent or happenstance or both—there was
what it was for me. The slant for him—my friend
the artist who set up situations—not lancing, as it
did not, or collapsing or draining the world into

flatness but making it full, rendering it ongoing and uncategorized and full. I myself felt less unfree inside his work.

Closed, I told myself again, beginning to gallop and then again to run, leaving behind the paralysis and the pipe in the wall, galloping and approaching something resembling, it had to be said, joy, was the problem, a closed question could be summarized, bringing things not into but fully past their meaning, making the world go flat. A closed question leading as it did to one place, leading as it was prone to always do to death. And death, too, organizing and summarizing, turning any object or work into a null thing, supplying the contours of itself, of death, death being the arrangement that would finally tell you—me—what your—my— work indeed was. Even as also however it was fully absurd, the absurdity of being alive and having to die was fully absurd, the absurdity of having to be, in the end, summarized and ordered and arranged into a null thing, but absurd was not the same as null, absurd to me being full seeming, a devouring or hollering, a devouring of the world as it presented itself ongoingly to me. Absurd or the spiral keeping things from coming fully into their meaning, good, said the spiral, there you are again. The truth about any object being that, looked at with a sort of slant, any object was an absurd object, there were eight million ways to be an absurd object, any object, looked at in the context of our absurdly finite lives, was an unreasonable object, not easy with being in the world.

Galloping and then running I saw that the way past death was to do anything I could to unfind the answer to the question of what my work was, to unaccept the fact of knowing the answer, to unknow, uncomplete, unaccept, unclose. I would unsolve for x, I would deny there was an x to be solved. I would arrange things to my dissatisfaction in all cases, every case would be the case, I would botch every transition, every border crossing, botching every border between categories or realms, dwelling in the botched transition, the hiccup, the glitch. I would plunge within limits and botch the limits, I would botch the pale, taunting and reneging on the pale and forcing things in and out of the network of things. I would misstep, I would loop and freely loop, I would make things difficult because difficult was how I made things.

This line of thinking was inconvenient, exhilarating. I had no idea what it might look like, I did not know but wanted, that is to say, to see. I was uneasy. I was uneasy! Galloping, hiccupping, I raced through the unlovely streets with the fugue as demented backdrop, looping back dementedly the long way toward the studio of my immaculately chaotic friend the well-known artist who set up situations. What a situation. I had to relay it to him immediately, in that immediate moment, I had to tell him about it, the whole story, the whole full story—the hoarse gallerist, the popped-out ceiling tile, the conjured printmaker, the noncommittal light. I would tell him how I had run through the grid to a familiar place and found chaos there, how I had traveled away from my syntax and got back with the loop or the spiral, the spiral taking me the long way, the loop getting me back. I ran, I ran, running however I thought I would be careful how I told it, the story. What was important was to not find the right words.

Thank you

to the interlocutors: Nate Lippens, Susan Robb,
Reed Anderson, Gretchen Gnaedinger, Davy
Knittle

to Claire Dederer, Andrea Geyer, Ellen Harvey,
Victoria Haven, Tricia Keightley, Tamara
Kostianovsky, Cornelius Severs, Guy Richards
Smit

to Tina Pohlman, Will Evans, Chad Post, Evan
Sult

to Walker Rutter-Bowman, Sara Balabanlilar,
Kirkby Gann Tittle

to the Halls, Redstones-Saltmarshes, and
Campbells, especially Phil and Mungo

to TB, JSB, GG, and all the artists who have
talked to me about what their work is

MICHAL AJVAZ, *The Golden Age.*
The Other City.

PIERRE ALBERT-BIROT, *Grabinoulor.*

YUZ ALESHKOVSKY, *Kangaroo.*

FELIPE ALFAU, *Chromos.*
Locos.

JOE AMATO, *Samuel Taylor's Last Night.*

IVAN ÂNGELO, *The Celebration.*
The Tower of Glass.

ANTÓNIO LOBO ANTUNES, *Knowledge of Hell.*
The Splendor of Portugal.

ALAIN ARIAS-MISSON, *Theatre of Incest.*

JOHN ASHBERY & JAMES SCHUYLER, *A Nest of Ninnies.*

ROBERT ASHLEY, *Perfect Lives.*

GABRIELA AVIGUR-ROTEM, *Heatwave and Crazy Birds.*

DJUNA BARNES, *Ladies Almanack.*
Ryder.

JOHN BARTH, *Letters.*
Sabbatical.

DONALD BARTHELME, *The King.*
Paradise.

SVETISLAV BASARA, *Chinese Letter.*

MIQUEL BAUÇÀ, *The Siege in the Room.*

RENÉ BELLETTO, *Dying.*

MAREK BIENCZYK, *Transparency.*

ANDREI BITOV, *Pushkin House.*

ANDREJ BLATNIK, *You Do Understand.*
Law of Desire.

LOUIS PAUL BOON, *Chapel Road.*
My Little War.
Summer in Termuren.

ROGER BOYLAN, *Killoyle.*

IGNÁCIO DE LOYOLA BRANDÃO, *Anonymous Celebrity.*
Zero.

BONNIE BREMSER, *Troia: Mexican Memoirs.*

CHRISTINE BROOKE-ROSE, *Amalgamemnon.*

BRIGID BROPHY, *In Transit.*
The Prancing Novelist.

GERALD L. BRUNS, *Modern Poetry and the Idea of Language.*

GABRIELLE BURTON, *Heartbreak Hotel.*

MICHEL BUTOR, *Degrees.*
Mobile.

G. CABRERA INFANTE, *Infante's Inferno.*
Three Trapped Tigers.

JULIETA CAMPOS, *The Fear of Losing Eurydice.*

ANNE CARSON, *Eros the Bittersweet.*

ORLY CASTEL-BLOOM, *Dolly City.*

LOUIS-FERDINAND CÉLINE, *North.*
Conversations with Professor Y.
London Bridge.

MARIE CHAIX, *The Laurels of Lake Constance.*

HUGO CHARTERIS, *The Tide Is Right.*

ERIC CHEVILLARD, *Demolishing Nisard.*
The Author and Me.

MARC CHOLODENKO, *Mordechai Schamz.*

JOSHUA COHEN, *Witz.*

EMILY HOLMES COLEMAN, *The Shutter of Snow.*

ERIC CHEVILLARD, *The Author and Me.*

ROBERT COOVER, *A Night at the Movies.*

STANLEY CRAWFORD, *Log of the S.S. The Mrs Unguentine.*
Some Instructions to My Wife.

RENÉ CREVEL, *Putting My Foot in It.*

RALPH CUSACK, *Cadenza.*

NICHOLAS DELBANCO, *Sherbrookes.*
The Count of Concord.

NIGEL DENNIS, *Cards of Identity.*

PETER DIMOCK, *A Short Rhetoric for Leaving the Family.*

ARIEL DORFMAN, *Konfidenz.*

COLEMAN DOWELL, *Island People.*
Too Much Flesh and Jabez.

ARKADII DRAGOMOSHCHENKO, *Dust.*

RIKKI DUCORNET, *Phosphor in Dreamland.*
The Complete Butcher's Tales.

RIKKI DUCORNET (cont.), *The Jade Cabinet*.
The Fountains of Neptune.

WILLIAM EASTLAKE, *The Bamboo Bed*.
Castle Keep.
Lyric of the Circle Heart.

JEAN ECHENOZ, *Chopin's Move*.

STANLEY ELKIN, *A Bad Man*.
Criers and Kibitzers, Kibitzers and Criers.
The Dick Gibson Show.
The Franchiser.
The Living End.
Mrs. Ted Bliss.

FRANÇOIS EMMANUEL, *Invitation to a Voyage*.

PAUL EMOND, *The Dance of a Sham*.

SALVADOR ESPRIU, *Ariadne in the Grotesque Labyrinth*.

LESLIE A. FIEDLER, *Love and Death in the American Novel*.

JUAN FILLOY, *Op Oloop*.

ANDY FITCH, *Pop Poetics*.

GUSTAVE FLAUBERT, *Bouvard and Pécuchet*.

KASS FLEISHER, *Talking out of School*.

JON FOSSE, *Aliss at the Fire*.
Melancholy.

FORD MADOX FORD, *The March of Literature*.

MAX FRISCH, *I'm Not Stiller*.
Man in the Holocene.

CARLOS FUENTES, *Christopher Unborn*.
Distant Relations.
Terra Nostra.
Where the Air Is Clear.

TAKEHIKO FUKUNAGA, *Flowers of Grass*.

WILLIAM GADDIS, JR., *The Recognitions*.

JANICE GALLOWAY, *Foreign Parts*.
The Trick Is to Keep Breathing.

WILLIAM H. GASS, *Life Sentences*.
The Tunnel.
The World Within the Word.
Willie Masters' Lonesome Wife.

GÉRARD GAVARRY, *Hoppla! 1 2 3*.

ETIENNE GILSON, *The Arts of the Beautiful*.
Forms and Substances in the Arts.

C. S. GISCOMBE, *Giscome Road*.
Here.

DOUGLAS GLOVER, *Bad News of the Heart*.

WITOLD GOMBROWICZ, *A Kind of Testament*.

PAULO EMÍLIO SALES GOMES, *P's Three Women*.

GEORGI GOSPODINOV, *Natural Novel*.

JUAN GOYTISOLO, *Count Julian*.
Juan the Landless.
Makbara.
Marks of Identity.

HENRY GREEN, *Blindness*.
Concluding.
Doting.
Nothing.

JACK GREEN, *Fire the Bastards!*

JIŘÍ GRUŠA, *The Questionnaire*.

MELA HARTWIG, *Am I a Redundant Human Being?*

JOHN HAWKES, *The Passion Artist*.
Whistlejacket.

ELIZABETH HEIGHWAY, ED., *Contemporary Georgian Fiction*.

AIDAN HIGGINS, *Balcony of Europe*.
Blind Man's Bluff.
Bornholm Night-Ferry.
Langrishe, Go Down.
Scenes from a Receding Past.

KEIZO HINO, *Isle of Dreams*.

KAZUSHI HOSAKA, *Plainsong*.

ALDOUS HUXLEY, *Antic Hay*.
Point Counter Point.
Those Barren Leaves.
Time Must Have a Stop.

NAOYUKI II, *The Shadow of a Blue Cat*.

DRAGO JANČAR, *The Tree with No Name*.

MIKHEIL JAVAKHISHVILI, *Kvachi*.

GERT JONKE, *The Distant Sound*.
Homage to Czerny.
The System of Vienna.

JACQUES JOUET, *Mountain R.*
Savage.
Upstaged.
MIEKO KANAI, *The Word Book.*
YORAM KANIUK, *Life on Sandpaper.*
ZURAB KARUMIDZE, *Dagny.*
JOHN KELLY, *From Out of the City.*
HUGH KENNER, *Flaubert, Joyce and Beckett: The Stoic Comedians.*
Joyce's Voices.
DANILO KIŠ, *The Attic.*
The Lute and the Scars.
Psalm 44.
A Tomb for Boris Davidovich.
ANITA KONKKA, *A Fool's Paradise.*
GEORGE KONRÁD, *The City Builder.*
TADEUSZ KONWICKI, *A Minor Apocalypse.*
The Polish Complex.
ANNA KORDZAIA-SAMADASHVILI, *Me, Margarita.*
MENIS KOUMANDAREAS, *Koula.*
ELAINE KRAF, *The Princess of 72nd Street.*
JIM KRUSOE, *Iceland.*
AYSE KULIN, *Farewell: A Mansion in Occupied Istanbul.*
EMILIO LASCANO TEGUI, *On Elegance While Sleeping.*
ERIC LAURRENT, *Do Not Touch.*
VIOLETTE LEDUC, *La Bâtarde.*
EDOUARD LEVÉ, *Autoportrait.*
Newspaper.
Suicide.
Works.
MARIO LEVI, *Istanbul Was a Fairy Tale.*
DEBORAH LEVY, *Billy and Girl.*
JOSÉ LEZAMA LIMA, *Paradiso.*
ROSA LIKSOM, *Dark Paradise.*
OSMAN LINS, *Avalovara.*
The Queen of the Prisons of Greece.
FLORIAN LIPUŠ, *The Errors of Young Tjaž.*
GORDON LISH, *Peru.*
ALF MACLOCHLAINN, *Out of Focus.*
Past Habitual.

The Corpus in the Library.
RON LOEWINSOHN, *Magnetic Field(s).*
YURI LOTMAN, *Non-Memoirs.*
D. KEITH MANO, *Take Five.*
MINA LOY, *Stories and Essays of Mina Loy.*
MICHELINE AHARONIAN MARCOM, *A Brief History of Yes.*
The Mirror in the Well.
BEN MARCUS, *The Age of Wire and String.*
WALLACE MARKFIELD, *Teitlebaum's Window.*
DAVID MARKSON, *Reader's Block.*
Wittgenstein's Mistress.
CAROLE MASO, *AVA.*
HISAKI MATSUURA, *Triangle.*
LADISLAV MATEJKA & KRYSTYNA POMORSKA, EDS., *Readings in Russian Poetics: Formalist & Structuralist Views.*
HARRY MATHEWS, *Cigarettes.*
The Conversions.
The Human Country.
The Journalist.
My Life in CIA.
Singular Pleasures.
The Sinking of the Odradek.
Stadium.
Tlooth.
HISAKI MATSUURA, *Triangle.*
DONAL MCLAUGHLIN, *beheading the virgin mary, and other stories.*
JOSEPH MCELROY, *Night Soul and Other Stories.*
ABDELWAHAB MEDDEB, *Talismano.*
GERHARD MEIER, *Isle of the Dead.*
HERMAN MELVILLE, *The Confidence-Man.*
AMANDA MICHALOPOULOU, *I'd Like.*
STEVEN MILLHAUSER, *The Barnum Museum.*
In the Penny Arcade.
RALPH J. MILLS, JR., *Essays on Poetry.*
MOMUS, *The Book of Jokes.*
CHRISTINE MONTALBETTI, *The Origin of Man.*
Western.

NICHOLAS MOSLEY, *Accident*.
Assassins.
Catastrophe Practice.
A Garden of Trees.
Hopeful Monsters.
Imago Bird.
Inventing God.
Look at the Dark.
Metamorphosis.
Natalie Natalia.
Serpent.

WARREN MOTTE, *Fables of the Novel: French Fiction since 1990*.
Fiction Now: The French Novel in the 21st Century.
Mirror Gazing.
Oulipo: A Primer of Potential Literature.

GERALD MURNANE, *Barley Patch*.
Inland.

YVES NAVARRE, *Our Share of Time*.
Sweet Tooth.

DOROTHY NELSON, *In Night's City*.
Tar and Feathers.

ESHKOL NEVO, *Homesick*.

WILFRIDO D. NOLLEDO, *But for the Lovers*.

BORIS A. NOVAK, *The Master of Insomnia*.

FLANN O'BRIEN, *At Swim-Two-Birds*.
The Best of Myles.
The Dalkey Archive.
The Hard Life.
The Poor Mouth.
The Third Policeman.

CLAUDE OLLIER, *The Mise-en-Scène*.
Wert and the Life Without End.

PATRIK OUŘEDNÍK, *Europeana*.
The Opportune Moment, 1855.

BORIS PAHOR, *Necropolis*.

FERNANDO DEL PASO, *News from the Empire*.
Palinuro of Mexico.

ROBERT PINGET, *The Inquisitory*.
Mahu or The Material.
Trio.

MANUEL PUIG, *Betrayed by Rita Hayworth*.

The Buenos Aires Affair.
Heartbreak Tango.

RAYMOND QUENEAU, *The Last Days*.
Odile.
Pierrot Mon Ami.
Saint Glinglin.

ANN QUIN, *Berg*.
Passages.
Three.
Tripticks.

ISHMAEL REED, *The Free-Lance Pallbearers*.
The Last Days of Louisiana Red.
Ishmael Reed: The Plays.
Juice!
The Terrible Threes.
The Terrible Twos.
Yellow Back Radio Broke-Down.

JASIA REICHARDT, *15 Journeys Warsaw to London*.

JOÃO UBALDO RIBEIRO, *House of the Fortunate Buddhas*.

JEAN RICARDOU, *Place Names*.

RAINER MARIA RILKE,
The Notebooks of Malte Laurids Brigge.

JULIÁN RÍOS, *The House of Ulysses*.
Larva: A Midsummer Night's Babel.
Poundemonium.

ALAIN ROBBE-GRILLET, *Project for a Revolution in New York*.
A Sentimental Novel.

AUGUSTO ROA BASTOS, *I the Supreme*.

DANIËL ROBBERECHTS, *Arriving in Avignon*.

JEAN ROLIN, *The Explosion of the Radiator Hose*.

OLIVIER ROLIN, *Hotel Crystal*.

ALIX CLEO ROUBAUD, *Alix's Journal*.

JACQUES ROUBAUD, *The Form of a City Changes Faster, Alas, Than the Human Heart*.
The Great Fire of London.
Hortense in Exile.
Hortense Is Abducted.
Mathematics: The Plurality of Worlds of Lewis.
Some Thing Black.

RAYMOND ROUSSEL, *Impressions of Africa.*

VEDRANA RUDAN, *Night.*

PABLO M. RUIZ, *Four Cold Chapters on the Possibility of Literature.*

GERMAN SADULAEV, *The Maya Pill.*

TOMAŽ ŠALAMUN, *Soy Realidad.*

LYDIE SALVAYRE, *The Company of Ghosts.*
The Lecture.
The Power of Flies.

LUIS RAFAEL SÁNCHEZ, *Macho Camacho's Beat.*

SEVERO SARDUY, *Cobra & Maitreya.*

NATHALIE SARRAUTE, *Do You Hear Them?*
Martereau.
The Planetarium.

STIG SÆTERBAKKEN, *Siamese.*
Self-Control.
Through the Night.

ARNO SCHMIDT, *Collected Novellas.*
Collected Stories.
Nobodaddy's Children.
Two Novels.

ASAF SCHURR, *Motti.*

GAIL SCOTT, *My Paris.*

DAMION SEARLS, *What We Were Doing and Where We Were Going.*

JUNE AKERS SEESE,
Is This What Other Women Feel Too?

BERNARD SHARE, *Inish.*
Transit.

VIKTOR SHKLOVSKY, *Bowstring.*
Literature and Cinematography.
Theory of Prose.
Third Factory.
Zoo, or Letters Not about Love.

PIERRE SINIAC, *The Collaborators.*

KJERSTI A. SKOMSVOLD,
The Faster I Walk, the Smaller I Am.

JOSEF ŠKVORECKÝ, *The Engineer of Human Souls.*

GILBERT SORRENTINO, *Aberration of Starlight.*
Blue Pastoral.
Crystal Vision.

Imaginative Qualities of Actual Things.
Mulligan Stew. Red the Fiend.
Steelwork.
Under the Shadow.

MARKO SOSIČ, *Ballerina, Ballerina.*

ANDRZEJ STASIUK, *Dukla.*
Fado.

GERTRUDE STEIN, *The Making of Americans.*
A Novel of Thank You.

LARS SVENDSEN, *A Philosophy of Evil.*

PIOTR SZEWC, *Annihilation.*

GONÇALO M. TAVARES, *A Man: Klaus Klump.*
Jerusalem.
Learning to Pray in the Age of Technique.

LUCIAN DAN TEODOROVICI,
Our Circus Presents…

NIKANOR TERATOLOGEN, *Assisted Living.*

STEFAN THEMERSON, *Hobson's Island.*
The Mystery of the Sardine.
Tom Harris.

TAEKO TOMIOKA, *Building Waves.*

JOHN TOOMEY, *Sleepwalker.*

DUMITRU TSEPENEAG, *Hotel Europa.*
The Necessary Marriage.
Pigeon Post.
Vain Art of the Fugue.

ESTHER TUSQUETS, *Stranded.*

DUBRAVKA UGRESIC, *Lend Me Your Character.*
Thank You for Not Reading.

TOR ULVEN, *Replacement.*

MATI UNT, *Brecht at Night.*
Diary of a Blood Donor.
Things in the Night.

ÁLVARO URIBE & OLIVIA SEARS, EDS.,
Best of Contemporary Mexican Fiction.

ELOY URROZ, *Friction.*
The Obstacles.

LUISA VALENZUELA, *Dark Desires and the Others.*
He Who Searches.

PAUL VERHAEGHEN, *Omega Minor.*

BORIS VIAN, *Heartsnatcher.*

LLORENÇ VILLALONGA, *The Dolls' Room.*

TOOMAS VINT, *An Unending Landscape.*

ORNELA VORPSI, *The Country Where No One Ever Dies.*

AUSTRYN WAINHOUSE, *Hedyphagetica.*

CURTIS WHITE, *America's Magic Mountain.*
The Idea of Home.
Memories of My Father Watching TV.
Requiem.

DIANE WILLIAMS,
Excitability: Selected Stories.
Romancer Erector.

DOUGLAS WOOLF, *Wall to Wall.*
Ya! & John-Juan.

JAY WRIGHT, *Polynomials and Pollen.*
The Presentable Art of Reading Absence.

PHILIP WYLIE, *Generation of Vipers.*

MARGUERITE YOUNG, *Angel in the Forest.*
Miss MacIntosh, My Darling.

REYOUNG, *Unbabbling.*

VLADO ŽABOT, *The Succubus.*

ZORAN ŽIVKOVIĆ , *Hidden Camera.*

LOUIS ZUKOFSKY, *Collected Fiction.*

VITOMIL ZUPAN, *Minuet for Guitar.*

SCOTT ZWIREN, *God Head.*

AND MORE . . .